HUSBAND FOR SALE

B.M. Hardin

Hardin Book Co.
www.authorbmhardin.com
ISBN: 978-1-7369437-2-4

Author Email: bmhardinbooks@gmail.com

Printed in the United States of America

This book is a work of fiction. Any similarities of people, places, instances, and locals are coincidental and solely a work of the author's imagination.

For Lamagea and T'yanna

HUSBAND FOR SALE

ONE

"I helped change your life. And now, you're going to help me become your husband's new wife."

A Few Months Earlier...

"Baby, I'm home," Alfonzo bellowed as soon as he opened the front door.

"Hey, baby," I puckered up my lips and awaited his warm, wet kiss. "Muah! How was your day?"

"Long and busy. I couldn't wait to get home to you."

"Um huh. You're such a charmer," I laughed.

"I'm serious, though. Shit, if I could put your cute little ass in my briefcase and take you to work with me I would," Al smirked, as he took a seat.

"First of all, there's nothing little about this ass, okay?"

"Oh, trust me. I know. Your ass is the main reason I married you."

"Hey!" Playfully I slapped Al's arm.

He laughed and so did I.

I placed my laptop on the coffee table as I stood up.

"Are you ready to eat?"

"Always." Al started to tug at my pink and gray pajama shorts.

"What are you doing?"

"You asked me if I was ready to eat," he smiled slyly.

"I was talking about dinner. I made your favorite. Spicy sausage chili and cornbread."

"Um huh," Al continued to tug at my shorts until my blush-colored thong was exposed.

"I think I want my dessert first," he kissed the bottom of my stomach. "I've been such a good boy. Can I have my dessert first, please?" He begged.

I knew that no matter what I said, Al wanted what he wanted. And he was going to get it.

Though I was only an hour away from a work deadline, as always, I let my husband have his way with me. That's what a good wife is supposed to do.

Right?

Don't get me wrong, sex with Al is good.

Over the years, he's moved from third to second place on my list of best sex I've ever had.

Unfortunately, my husband will never be number one.

No one, and I do mean no one, could ever take the place of the one and the only: Draco Saint Peterson.

Draco was my first live-in, long-term relationship.

And a demon with good dick.

That man was everything your mama warned you about; plus his dick was made of gold with a little bit of crack cocaine in it.

Draco's "devil dick" is the only addiction I've ever had to face and overcome. And I'll be the first to admit that it wasn't easy.

His dick wasn't too big, and it surely wasn't small, but I'm willing to bet any amount of money that he has one of the best dicks on God's green earth!

Draco had what the old folks call "Dick of Amnesia".

He could lie, cheat, raise hell all day, bring my car back on E, and spend all my money, but when the lights were off, and the panties came sliding down...

I got amnesia.

Everything, anything, he'd done prior to putting that *thing* inside me was simply forgiven and with each stroke, quickly forgotten.

And as expected, really good dick comes with drama and it's almost always attached to a man who isn't worth a damn!

After Draco cheated on me for what had to be the twentieth time, and a crazy lady showing up at my house trying to get her next *fix* from him, I realized that I had to let him go.

I shivered at the thought of how Draco used to make me feel. Sex with him was a high that I've never quite experienced again, and I don't think I would want to.

I can't afford to be another man's fool.

Shaking away my thoughts, I managed to focused on the matter at hand---sex with my darling husband.

It doesn't take much to get Al going.

The more I participate, the faster he'll cum, so I gave Al the best ten minutes of his life, leaving him on the couch satisfied and pretending to smoke a cigarette.

"Thank you, baby," Al said as I reached him a plate of food and a cold glass of sweet tea a few minutes later.

"You're welcome," I took a seat at the end of the couch. "Now, I have all of twenty-minutes to finish this product description for one of our new pieces and publish it on the company's website."

I'm an artist.

But currently, I work for the largest auction house on the East Coast to pay the bills.

Well, not really.

Al pays the bills; all of them.

All I do is buy groceries and toilet paper.

And my husband barely wants me to do that.

Al is old school.

He's definitely the type of husband who provides and protects. He's so manly, and he will try to fix anything just to show me how strong and useful he is.

Al is also what most people might call a geek.

But boy does he make geek look good!

My husband has the smoothest almond colored skin I've ever seen. Big lips, dark eyes, and a full scruffy beard.

Al is muscular in all the right places, and he has a crooked yet sort of mesmerizing smile. And he's one of the smartest people I know. He works for a fairly well-known tech company in downtown Savannah. And most of the time, I have no idea what he's talking about, but I smile and pretend to listen.

"Do your thing, baby. I'm going to eat and finish up a few things myself," Al smacked his lips.

Ugh!

I hate the way he chews!

Al's chomping irritated the hell out of me, making it hard to focus, but somehow, I was able to finish the product description and press publish two minutes before the deadline.

"Finished!"

Al didn't respond.

He now had his laptop in his hands, and I knew that I would be completely invisible to him for the next hour or so.

Good.

Marriage is hard.

Even when you have an amazing husband like Al.

Al does everything right.

I couldn't have prayed for a better husband.

Seriously, he really is a great guy.

It's just some days, sometimes…

I wish I was free.

Alfonzo and I met five years ago at a karaoke bar across the street from my old job.

My sister Sophie and I were singing "Mustang Sally" on stage, and I spotted Al in the front row.

He was laughing.

He noticed me looking at him, and after smirking at me, he took a sip of his drink and winked.

Once I was off stage, Al didn't hesitate to follow me to the bar.

Honestly, I was surprised he even noticed me at all standing next to Sophie…

The bombshell.

I've always been the brains.

Sophie has always been and still is the beauty.

I guess if you go by society's standards.

My sister, Sophie, is one of the prettiest women I have ever seen. She has the height and face of a runway model. And the body of a perfectly sculpted statue on display at a museum.

She's about 5'10" with flawless honey brown skin. She has a body full of perfect curves and a flat stomach. Sophie's cheekbones are so bold and precise, and they draw attention to her perfect nose. She has some of the cutest dimples and an amazing smile that lights up the darkest of rooms. Sophie has big, beautiful brown and hazel eyes, surrounded by long, thick natural eyelashes. And a head full of natural ebony curls.

And even with all that said, she's probably about ten times more gorgeous than I could ever describe.

I'm a little more, uh, let's just say basic.

Sophie and I have the same beautiful coils, but other than that, I'm just an average light brown-skinned girl.

I have wide hips and juicy thighs that clap when I walk. My eyes are brown, and my nose is slightly too big for my face. My stomach only appears to be flat when I wear my girdle, but it's far from it. Though, I did get a nice set of boobs and a nice, round ass.

But like I said, for the most part, I'm just all around normal looking. Nothing too special about me. I look like our dad. Sophie got the beautiful genes of our mom and grandmother.

But Al noticed me.

That night, Sophie thought Al was approaching the bar to talk to her but instead, he looked directly at me and asked to buy me a drink.

The rest was pretty much a breeze from there.

Al gave life a whole new meaning.

Al made life fun and easy.

He was sweet, kind, and gentle with me.

And he took me on some of the most memorable dates and trips of my life! Al took me to New York for my birthday. We spent one Christmas in Africa. He cooked for me, often, and we went on picnics on the beach, as well as in the park.

Al took me skiing and skydiving, which were both on my bucket list. He was always encouraging me to try new things. Al showered me with the love that I've always longed for. The love I never knew I needed or deserved.

And our second-year anniversary of dating, Al flew me to Paris and proposed to me in front of a few members of our families and friends.

We married a year later, and our second-year wedding anniversary is only two months away.

I love Al.

I really do.

But like I said…

Marriage is hard.

My husband is so good to me, and yet some days, I would rather him not be. Some days, I would prefer to be alone. Some days, I wish I didn't have to cater to anyone else. Some days, I wish we would argue so I could make him sleep in the guest bedroom, just to have our new king-sized bed all to myself.

Some days, I just want to be breathe.

Some days, I just want to be selfishly all about me.

Some days.

I majored in art, with a minor in business in college.

Painting, drawing and creating is my superpower.

And marketing is the cherry on top.

I can sell just about anything, which is how I ended up working at the auction house.

I enjoy my job.

I honestly do.

It's good money.

But I want to get back to my passion and creating my own art. I want to get back to the things I love.

It's just lately, I've been so busy, and I feel so uninspired.

When I first started dating Al, I painted two of the most amazing pieces of my life. I sold both pieces to one of Al's previous neighbors for $1,500 each.

I was so proud!

And not to mention, shocked, that she would pay that much for my work, but I knew that it was only the beginning.

I continued to create, but I wanted a more stable income, so, I snagged the job at the auction house the same year Al proposed to me.

But being around such amazing pieces of art, five days a week, makes me burn with the constant desire to paint and create pieces of my own, yet I can never seem to find the right inspiration these days.

It's just not as easy as it used to be.

Have you ever wanted to do something, with all your heart, and you just can't?

You know that you have the skills and the capability but for whatever reason, you can't do the one thing you want to do more than anything in the world.

Let me tell you, it's the worst feeling ever!

All I want to do is draw, paint, stroke a paintbrush here, draw a person or two there, but I just can't.

And I think it's because I'm always so focused on being the perfect wife to a perfect husband.

Or maybe it's just me.

With Al working in the living room, and with my passion on my mind, I headed downstairs to our fully furnished basement, which is also my art studio.

"Okay, Nema, come on! Paint something great," I gave myself a pep talk.

After placing on an apron, and pulling my hair up in a bun, I took a seat on my favorite stool.

For a few minutes, I stared at the blank canvas.

I tried to channel my feelings and emotions as I chewed on the end of my lucky paintbrush.

"Red. I'm feeling red," I dabbed my paintbrush in the red paint. "Nope." I frowned after one stroke. "Yellow. Let's try yellow."

Needless to say, all I did was sit there, waste time and make one big, colorful ass mess!

"Maybe I should draw something first."

I headed to my desk. I picked up my sketching pencil and with the tip of the pencil pressed down hard against the paper, I sat there.

And I sat there. And I sat just a little while longer.

Ugh!

See, I'm broken!

Why can't I draw anything?

Why can't I paint something?

I've never had this problem before.

I can remember getting out of bed in the middle of the night just to paint something that I'd dreamt about.

I remember the days I would be driving or simply sitting in a coffee shop and I'd rush home full of inspiration and ideas.

Where did it all go?

Where's the creativeness when I need it the most?

I'm not sure how long I sat looking at the blank page, in deep thought, but it was to no surprise of mine I heard…

"Baby! What are you doing?" Al yelled from the top of the basement stairs. "Our show is about to come on. And you know I can't watch it without you. Come on! Hurry!"

I exhaled softly. "Coming!"

I placed the pencil down and stood up feeling heavy.

Feeling something that I've been feeling a lot lately.

Feeling like my passion is gone.

Something is wrong.

"Baby!" I heard Al yell from the living room just as I made it to the top of the stairs.

Feeling defeated, I frowned in failure as I cut off the light and closed the basement door behind me.

~***~

"Look who finally decided to show up at work," Vanessa smirked.

"I'm literally only one minute late," I groaned. "And I'm never late. I'm always early."

"I know. That's why I'm always counting on you to get here first to do the shit that I don't want to do," she laughed.

Vanessa is my manager---but only in title.

Most days, I do her job and mine.

Basically, I make her look good.

Too good, sometimes.

The only reason I let it slide is because she has also become my feisty, Spanish-speaking, friend. And because unlike her, I don't plan on being here forever.

Someday, my artwork is going to make me famous.

It's going to take me places.

I know that I have a million-dollar talent.

And somehow, I have to figure out how to start using it again.

"Connie will be here today, so, I'll be around a lot more than usual."

"Of course, you will."

Connie is part owner of Shauna Bella's Auction House.

Connie is what some might call crazy, stupid, rich!

She and her business partner, Giselle, have been featured on the cover of so many magazines, raving of their beauty and financial success.

Two black girls.

One goal. One dream. And they did it!

They made Shauna Bella's bigger than either of them could've ever imagined, bringing in millions of dollars in profit over the past seven years.

"Well, I guess I'll get out here and at least look like I'm working," Vanessa smiled.

I took a moment to adore some of the new paintings that had recently arrived and would be auctioned off soon.

The details and the colors of each painting consumed me. Staring at them, touching them, made me feel all warm and fuzzy inside.

I attempted to guess the inspiration behind each of them. I wondered what the artist was feeling. I wanted to know what they were thinking with each stroke of their paintbrush. I wanted to know how they came up with the name of their painting, and I stared at each painting wondering if I would've named it something else.

"There you are," I heard her chipper voice behind me.

"Hi, Mrs. Connie. How are you doing?" I asked her as she hugged me.

Connie is in her early forties, but she doesn't look a day older than twenty-nine. I guess when you have the type of money she has, you can make yourself look as young as you want to.

Her skin is brown and completely flawless.

Her face is slimmer than it should be for its features. Connie always wears red lipstick, and her teeth are a blinding white and perfectly straight. She wears long, lustrous weave, and her body is perfectly proportioned as though she's had a surgery or two.

"I'm doing great. I see you've been keeping everything in order around here. I know Vanessa's lazy ass doesn't deserve the credit."

I chuckled. "She does some things…sometimes."

"Um huh. I bet."

Connie has always made it crystal clear that she's quite fond of me. She gave me the job after only interviewing me for three minutes. Once, she told me that I remind her of herself. She told me that working for her company would only be temporary because I'm destined for greater.

I used to believe her.

These days, I'm not so sure.

"So, what's new? Have you been creating? Drawing? Painting? Whatever you're up to, I'm sure it's gorgeous! And you know you can always put it up to be auctioned off here. Just let me see it first, just in case I want to purchase it for myself."

"Ugh, I haven't been able to do much of anything lately. And I've tried. Sometimes I'm down in my basement, for hours, and I just can't seem to get anything done."

"Don't worry. Most artist go through this at some time or another. One day, you'll wake up and suddenly be full of creativity! So much so that you won't be able to stop drawing or painting even if you tried!"

"I hope so."

Connie made her exit.

I started to think about one of my favorite art professors in college.

Madeline Barclay.

She isn't a famous artist or anything, but she very well should be. Her work is phenomenal!

I would stay after class just to have one on one time with her. She would allow me to sit and watch her paint for hours. She taught me so many tips and tricks, and she told me that I had more than just talent. She said I had a gift.

"Let's take a break," Vanessa interrupted my thoughts.

"A break? We just got here."

"And?"

I shook my head. "I can see your future."

"What? What about my future?"

"Unemployment."

Vanessa giggled as she joined me at my side to start tagging inventory.

Well…

She tagged two or three things.

And then, she watched me tag the rest.

~***~

"So, I met a new guy…"

"Again? Isn't this like the fifth guy this year?" I questioned my sister, Sophie.

"More like tenth," our older brother, Cameron teased.

"Nema, shut up. And Cam…fuck you," Sophie laughed. "But seriously, you guys, I really like this one."

"You said that last time…"

"Well, everyone can't be as lucky as you are, Nema! You have Mr. Alfonzo. The perfect husband."

I remained silent.

He is pretty perfect.

"I thought you were going to focus on your boutique?" Cam asked.

Sophie owns a very successful boutique in Savannah, Georgia. She brings in five to six figures, a month, and nothing in her store is under $100.

And I do mean nothing!

"I am focused on my boutique and expanding. But a girl still needs love."

"Dick," I corrected her. "You said love, but I'm sure you meant to say dick."

"No…yes…I mean, ugh!" Sophie huffed as Cam and I howled in laughter. "I do want to get married one day, too, you know. I want to be like both of you. Married. And two or three kids wouldn't hurt either. I can't wait to have a little mini-me!"

I could tell by the look on my sister's face that she was serious.

"Sophie, you'll have everything you want. Don't rush it. You have a pretty amazing life right now. Honestly, I admire you. No matter what, you go after what you want. And you don't care what anyone has to say about it. So, if love is what you want, there's no doubt in my mind that you won't have it."

"Okay, okay," Cam bellowed. "Can we go now, or what?"

Sophie locked up her boutique, and the Reid Kids headed across the street to this new Italian spot for dinner.

Our parents, Marvin and Darla Reid, passed away in a car accident when I was sixteen and Sophie was fifteen.

Cam was twenty-two and newly married, but he and his wife took us in. They finished raising us. They got me off to college and the next year, Sophie went off to hair school, although she didn't finish.

And finally, Cam and his wife, Venus, were able to start their own family. They're the proud parents of my three handsome nephews; Cameron Junior, Cory, and Carter.

I have so much respect for my brother Cam.

He's a good guy.

Hardworking, talented. Funny.

In some ways, he reminds me of my husband.

Cam could've turned his back on us, but he didn't.

And one day, I plan to repay him.

In a way, Sophie already has.

When her boutique started bringing in tons of cash, she sent Cam and his wife on an exotic honeymoon, and then she surprised our brother and his family with a brand-new house, allowing him to finally put our parent's old house up for sale.

Al and I make plenty of money, together, but surely not enough to buy my brother a $350,000 house in cash.

But one day, I'll be able to show him just how much he means to me, too.

"Dinner is on me tonight," Cam said. "Order whatever y'all want. Nema, get yourself a drink or two. You seem tensed."

"Not tensed. Just a lot on my mind. I haven't been able to paint anything lately and it's driving me crazy!"

"Really?" Sophie asked. "You've never had a problem being creative before."

"I know. That's why it's driving me crazy! I need some kind of inspiration."

"Good dick usually inspires me. Are you and Al having sex? And not the boring, married people kind. I'm talking about hot, kinky, freaky, porno-type sex," Sophie laughed.

"Excuse me?" I rolled my eyes. "He gets it whenever he wants it, if you must know. And I always put it down in the bedroom, okay? Every single time," I lied.

It's been a while since I've been in the mood for some freaky shit with my husband. I'm sure it's because he never gives me a chance to come on to him. He always wants it. So, I just give him what he wants, and go on about my day.

"Hey, hey, hey," Cam said disgusted.

"Well, I'm all out of ideas," Sophie shrugged.

I giggled at her response.

Viewing our surroundings, every man, at every single table, within ten feet of ours, sat gawking at Sophie.

Even the men who were with their wives and girlfriends.

Cam noticed it too, and we both started to chuckle.

"What?" Sophie asked, totally oblivious to her surroundings. Or maybe she was just used to it.

"Nothing."

Her beauty really is something else.

Especially when you see her for the first time.

And the way she dresses draws even more attention to herself.

Sophie is wearing a bright red, strapless dress. It's skintight, and it literally stops just an inch or so past her ass. Meanwhile, I'm sitting across from her dressed like a 1982 grandma, with the exception of my stylish sexy open-toed leather shoes.

That's another clear sign that I haven't been feeling like myself lately. If nothing else, I like to look good. I have tons of cute plus-size clothes.
I love to dress sexy.

But here lately, I've been dressing more for comfort than anything else. Most days, I don't even bother to comb my hair. I just put it in a bun and go on about my day.

I touched my earlobes noticing that I'd gone all day without wearing earrings.

"I don't know about y'all," Sophie started. "But since Cam is paying…I'm about to get me a drink…or five!"

It's not often that the three of us are able to get together, but when we do, it's always a great time.

Dinner with my brother and sister was everything I needed and more. We laughed and reminisced. We even managed to talk about our parents without getting emotional.

We had great parents.

I was always a daddy's girl.

Our father was the perfect example of what a father and a husband is supposed to be. He would sometimes joke that I was more of a son than Cam was. And it was because I wanted to do any and everything that he did.

To this day, I can fix almost anything underneath the hood of a car, change a flat tire in six-inch heels, and grill like nobody's business; although I don't do any of these things anymore because Al does them all.

Our mother made sure that all of us knew how to cook. She used to tell Sophie and I that the way to a man's heart is through his stomach. And she would also tell Cam that a man cooking a meal or two every once in a while, could save a marriage.

To this day, Cam can cook just about anything.

And if I'm being honest, he cooks ten times better than his wife.

Our parents did as best as they could to prepare us for the world. They always told us that they wanted each of us to have, if nothing but a piece, of what they had with each other.

Our parents love was healthy.

It was equal.

It was everlasting.

It was only fit that they died together because I don't think one could have survived without the other.

They were perfect.

Individually.

But most definitely, together.

I found myself staring at Sophie's new tattoo.

Sophie probably has at least fifteen tattoos.

All very small.

And all in random places.

All absolutely meaningless to her.

I only have one.

The infinity symbol.

Al and I got matching tattoos last year on our first anniversary.

"Cute tattoo, Soph."

"Oh, thank you. Surprisingly, it hurt like hell," she smiled at the tattoo of a purple ladybug on the knuckle of her right thumb. "It took me forever to decide on what insect to get. I refused to get a butterfly. That's so…normal." At the buzz of her cell phone, Sophie glanced down at the table. Immediately, she frowned, but quickly replaced her frown with a smile as though she didn't want us to know that something was wrong.

Sophie hasn't introduced us to a man of hers in a very long time. She's rarely in a serious relationship, and when she is, she's so secretive about it for some reason or another.

If you ask me, and though her lifestyle would suggest otherwise, Sophie is the bigger romantic out of the three of us. No one wants what our parents had more than she does.

My cell phone chimed.

Instead of texting Al back, I tuned into what Sophie started to blabber about for the next thirty minutes.

Listening to one of her crazy stories, made me think about some of the crazy situations I've been in myself.

My last year of college, I started to sleep around with one of the college professors. He wasn't one of my teachers, but still, we weren't supposed to be fooling around. Nevertheless, he never told me that he was actually in a relationship with someone else.

One night, at his house off campus, as he ate my pussy on his cherry oak kitchen table, someone started to bang on the front door.

The professor went to see who it was. He came back into the kitchen with a dumb look on his face, and then her said:

"If I were you…I would hide."

I forced him to explain.

Needless to say, he explained that he had a crazy girlfriend, who was banging on his front door with a bat in her hand. Apparently, she had been questioning him lately about cheating on her, and she was popping up to see if she could catch him.

I ended up hiding in a closet, butt naked, with chocolate sauce on my titties, and whipped cream all over my pussy, for over three hours.

And once he opened the closet door, I'd tried to slap the mustache off his face for putting me in that situation.

I got dressed, and just as we were about to get into his car, so he could drop me back off at the college, his crazy girlfriend swerved into the driveway behind us.

Long story short, her crazy ass chased me with a bat for three blocks. And I never so much as glanced at the professor again.

"We have to do this again, soon," Cam embraced both Sophie and I, at the same time, with his big, chocolate beefy arms as soon as we walked out of the restaurant.

Cam has always been a big man just like our father was.

"Uh um," both Sophie and I turned around at the sound of a man clearing his throat behind us.

Instantaneously, Sophie smiled.

"Uh, I'll talk to you guys later. Love y'all!" Sophie walked towards the well-dressed man wearing an expensive suit.

"Wait, I thought you just met…"

"Bye, Nema!" Sophie interrupted my sentence, as she grabbed the gentleman by the arm and strutted away.

"Don't hurt him now!" Cam yelled playfully behind her. "That girl is something else."

"She's a mess!" I laughed. "A beautiful, fearless, reckless mess!"

Cam shared a chuckle or two with me before abruptly asking me a question.

"Are you okay, Nema? Like really okay?"

I nodded. "Yeah. I'm okay. I think. Just work and stuff. You know?"

"Yeah. I do know." Cam agreed. "And how is my boy, Al?"

"He's fine." I gave my brother a goodbye kiss on his right cheek. "He's as perfect as always."

Twenty minutes later, I arrived at my two-story home in Richmond Hills. Immediately, I noticed the freshly cut lawn. I smiled at the thought of Al riding on his brand-new lawnmower, in the hot July sun, still in his work clothes.

Inside my head, I could hear him humming his favorite tune. That man is obsessed with Gerald Levert and pretty much every male R&B singer from that era.

And he's a pretty good singer too.

Whenever I'm sick, Al holds me in his arms, and sings to me until I fall asleep.

I should feel lucky to be Al's wife.

And I do.

At least I did.

No. I still do.

I think.

I'm so confused!

And I really need to get it together!

I would hate to lose a good man like Al and end up with a liar, cheater...or a man like my ex.

A few months before meeting Al, I was in a relationship with a man named Wendell for about a year.

On paper, he's a pretty good catch.

Great career.

Educated.

Handsome and Athletic.

Never married and he didn't have any kids.

But in reality...

A pill or two a day, keeps the crazy away!

That man had it all...except a diagnosis!

It all started out of nowhere about eight months into our relationship.

He wasn't physically abusive or anything, but some days, he would call me other people's names, bite on himself whenever he got upset, and change his voice, like in some random accent for 24-hour periods at a time.

I found it all funny, at first, because I thought he was joking and doing it all on purpose, until one day, I realized that he just might actually be crazy!

Once, he talked like a corporate white woman all day long. He would even snap at me and tell me to have a report on his desk by the end of the day. And no matter how mad I became, he would tell me to loosen the fuck up in his regular voice, and then change it back to the white woman's voice again.

Needless to say, I hauled ass on him, and I never looked back.

And then…

I met Al.

Normal, adventurous, faithful, hardworking Al.

He's almost too good to be true, and I'll admit that for the first few months, I kept waiting on something to happen. I waited for him to change or for him to give me a red flag, but he never did. To this day, he's the same man that I met five years ago.

After sitting in my car for a little while longer, finally, I made my way inside.

I found Al in the bedroom halfway asleep.

"Hey, baby," he smiled at me.

"Hey, handsome."

"How was your day? How was dinner with Sophie and Cam?"

"It was great," I stepped out of my shoes.

"Come here. Let me rub your feet."

"Oh, yes, I really need that."

I hopped onto the bed, as Al chuckled and grabbed my right foot.

"Work is going to be so busy tomorrow. I really need to get a good nights' rest. We have so many new pieces that need to be catalogued and priced for our big auction at the end of the month."

"You got this, babe. You'll get everything ready. They would be lost without you."

"Thank you, baby. Oooh, yes, right there," I closed my eyes to enjoy Al's magic fingers as they danced all over the bottom of my foot. "I really, really needed this foot rub."

"I can tell," Al chuckled. "If you stop trying to squeeze these big ass feet in those little ass shoes…"

"Uh, uh, don't come for me or my shoes, okay?" I laughed.

"Okay," Al gave me a genuine smile just before saying his next sentence. "Why don't you go on and take a shower. We can continue this when you get out."

Translation…

"Go wash your ass so you can fuck me!"

That's not what he said, but that's exactly what he meant.

"Okay," I held my breath until I was inside the bathroom. Finally, I exhaled.

I turned on the shower but spent the first few minutes sitting on the toilet.

My mind started to race.

Thoughts of work, painting, Al and even Sophie flooded my mind.

I wondered what Sophie was doing or if she was *doing* the guy from the restaurant. I frowned after realizing I hadn't brought my cell phone into the bathroom with me.

Sophie has always been promiscuous.

She's always done exactly whatever, and whoever she wants to do, and she does it unapologetically.

Even when some things, or should I say, some people should be off limits.

I can remember her driving Cam crazy during her junior and senior year of high school.

It was hard trying to tame her.

Cam and Sophie argued all the time, almost every day. It would scare me sometimes, especially when Sophie would tell him she hated him, or remind him that he wasn't our father. I would wonder if she made Cam want to give up on her, on us, but he never did.

Often, I would catch Cam talking to himself.

Once, I heard him say: "I just have to get her across that stage. I gotta' do this for Mama and Daddy. I can't give up on her. I can do this."

And he did it.

He got Sophie through high school and even convinced her to go to hair school; although she only made it halfway through before realizing that she wasn't as in to doing hair as she thought she was.

For a few years, Sophie struggled to find her place in the world. And then, she finally got the idea to open a boutique. I actually loaned her the ten-grand from my savings account at the time to get her boutique off the ground. She paid me back only three months after the boutique opened.

From the very beginning, I knew Sophie's boutique was going to be a success.

Sophie is such a people-person, and she knows how to use her beauty and her booty to her advantage; especially when it comes to making money.

Now, Sophie is living out her dreams and I'm so proud of her.

She's successful.

She's happy.

She's free.

And if I'm being honest, in some ways, I wish I was her.

"Baby!" Al yelled. Are you still in the shower?"

I didn't answer my husband.

Instead, I flushed the toilet and undressed.

The scorching hot water instantly eased my troubled mind. With my eyes closed, I thought about my wedding day.

It was perfect.

Small and intimate.

The weather was amazing for a beautiful September day, and I remember the exact look on Al's face as Cam led me towards him.

He looked so happy.

He looked so sure.

Word for word, I still remember Al's wedding vows.

"Nema, you gave my life a whole new meaning. Before you, I was just existing. Today, I'm the luckiest man on earth because now I get to spend the rest of my life, existing with you. Every day with you is a gift. And I promise to spend the rest of my life showing you and God how much I appreciate the gift that he has given me. I will never let you down. I will never let you fall. I will never stop loving you. You are everything, and I mean everything I've ever wanted in a woman, and if I'm dreaming, please don't wake me. Let me stay right here, in this dream, with you. Forever.

Those are the words Al said to me on our wedding day.

And there's no doubt in my mind that he hadn't meant every, single one of them.

I know that Al will always love and take care of me.

And whether I like it or not, I vowed to do the same.

"Baby!"

I washed my body in a hurry.

Duty calls.

And it's my duty, to give my husband this booty.

I guess.

~***~

"Those bags under your eyes aren't cute," Diana smirked.

"And neither is your face. Or those shoes. So, I guess that makes us even."

Diana rolled her eyes.

Diana has only been working at the auction house for about a year, if that long. She and I have the same title, and we have this sort of love-hate relationship.

Sometimes we get along.

Other times, she seems to be in competition with me. She's almost always in a bad mood, and she's just an overall negative person. Definitely one of those people that you feed with a long-handled spoon, and most definitely a person that you avoid and ignore outside of work.

"Are you ready?" Diana said.

"Always."

And with that, we both walked out onto the auction stage to start our monthly live auction.

I smiled at the room of about a hundred eager faces.

There's millions, possibly billions of dollars in this room, and they're all ready to spend money on valuable pieces of art, one-of-a-kind jewelry, and other expensive merchandise.

Let the bidding begin!

"Nema? Nema Reid, is that you?"

I turned around.

Immediately, I recognized one of my college classmates and old friend.

"Lula Lineberger? Oh my goodness! And it's Nema McCoy now."

Lula smiled. "And it's Lula Montgomery, now. Although I should probably change my name back since I'm divorced."

We both chuckled as we embraced each other.

"How are you?"

"I'm doing well. Divorced. Rich. You know, nothing much," Lula laughed. "And you? I guess I can see how you ended up working here, but I was sure you would be some kind of famous artist, living in Europe somewhere, by now. You were a bad ass with the paintbrush. Your work was always so good."

Lula and I were both art majors in college.

Most of our classes were together, which is how we ended up becoming pretty good friends.

Lula is only about five feet tall and as high-yellow as the sun. She's also as flat chested as a boy, but her big ole' booty surely makes up for it.

Lula has always had a big, country ass. Her ass is even bigger than mine. She has one of those asses that you can see it from the front, and it jiggles like Jell-O when she walks.

Back in the day, Lula was loud, and some might even say a little ghetto. She was always the life of the party.

Adventurous.

Spontaneous.

Completely out of control.

But she was also a little on the bougie side.

It's to no surprise of mine that Lula married a man with money. In college, she was always spending money she didn't have. She was always rich, inside her head, and she even convinced me to get two credit cards that took me over five years to pay back.

Lula was always putting me up to something, but I liked it, in a way. She helped me to come out of my shell and she taught me that it was okay to grow, change, and adapt when necessary.

She also taught me that it's okay to experiment.

Lula was a firm believer that a person should do a little bit of this, and try a little bit of that, in order to figure out what they really like.

Listening to Lula, I ended up in a threesome, once.

Lula always told such exciting sex stories.

She was a lot like my sister, Sophie, and I'm sure that's why I was drawn to her.

She was always screwing somebody.

Whether it was her man, or someone else's.

Nevertheless, one night, after telling me about her wild sex escapades, Lula told me that college was the place to explore and try new things.

So...

At the time, there was a guy who often showed interest in me. I remember walking to his dorm room that night. My heart was beating faster than a SR-71 jet.

I chose him for my threesome experience because though he was interested in me, his roommate was more my type.

So, I knocked on the door and I made it clear that I wanted him---and his friend.

Long story short...

I did it.

I tried it.

And I'll never admit this again, but I actually liked it.

To this very day, Lula, is the only person that I've ever told about that night.

I'm not sure when or how Lula and I lost touch after graduation. I would've thought we'd be lifelong friends, but somewhere along the way, the phone calls and emails stopped coming.

And Lula was simply forgotten.

Until now.

"Thank you. And I'm still an artist. This job just sort of fell into my lap. And what about you? You were pretty good with the paintbrush yourself."

"I can't tell you the last time I picked up a paintbrush," Lula frowned. "And I strongly doubt I will ever paint again," she shrugged. "Shortly after college, I met this guy. He pretended to be a regular guy, but he ended up being rich! And I mean…loaded! He married me and we lived out in L.A. I had everything I ever wanted. I was living the good life. And then, after several years of marriage, I found out he was sleeping with his finance manager's assistant. Long story short, I divorced him, got half of everything, and moved back down here to the South. I just purchased my second home, which is why I came to this auction today to find some unique pieces to put into it."

Lula opened up her newly released turquoise and lavender Chanel bag.

"Here's my card. I know what kind of talent you have, so if you create something that you think I'll be interested in, give me a call. I'll pay whatever your price is. It was good seeing you, Nema."

Lula walked away as Diana approached me.

"You know her?"

"Yes. We went to college together."

"Oh, well, you should've followed in her footsteps. She's the one who purchased that two-million-dollar painting of the slave girl; the one with the sunflowers. Homegirl is paid!"

Just before Lula walked out of the auction house, she looked back at me and winked her eye.

And in that moment, I knew that somehow, and in some way, Lula was about to play a major part in changing my life.

Forever.

****

TWO

"You look amazing, baby!" Al complimented me.

"Thank you. Are you ready to go?"

"Yep."

We were headed out for our monthly date night with Al's friends, who had also become pretty good friends of mine over the years.

Al has two best friends: Paul, who is married to Gia. And Jack, who is married to Cathy.

And we all get together at least once a month for dinner.

Al, Paul and Jack have been best friends since elementary school. They are as close as brothers, and honestly, Al may love them just a little bit more than his actual siblings.

The three men also went to college together, and they all work in the same field. I've always wanted friends like the ones Al has, and I feel pretty lucky at times to have married into the tribe.

Fifteen minutes later, Al and I arrived at the restaurant.

"Oooh, I love that dress!" Paul's wife, Gia said as she kissed my cheek.

"Thank you. Hey, lady," I said kissing the cheek of Cathy, Jack's wife.

"Hey, honey!"

Al pulled out my chair and we sat down to what we knew was going to be a great time.

"Well, Jack and I have an announcement," Cathy said just as dinner was being placed on the table. Jack grabbed her hand. "We're uh…we're getting a divorced."

"What?" I asked aloud.

Everyone started to talk at once.

Finally, Jack's voice overpowered everyone else's.

"We don't hate each other. We love each other. We're just not in love with each other anymore. A divorce is what's best for us."

"Hell, since y'all are telling it, we may as well too," Gia said out of nowhere. "Paul and I filed for divorce last week. We've been living separate for almost a year. We've just been pretending to live together and just kept coming to these dinners."

I studied Al's face.

I couldn't tell if he was in shock or hurt.

It's quite obvious that both of his best friends have been hiding their marital statuses from him.

"We just grew a part after that last miscarriage and we never found our way back to each other. So, we're divorcing. And we're both pretty happy about it." Paul exhaled.

"Looks like this will be our last group dinner," Gia shrugged. "So, let's get drunk and enjoy the night. Shall we?"

We all raised our glasses.

All of them were smiling.

Our friends are getting a divorce.

And they seem completely content and at peace with their decisions.

They don't hate each other.

They're not embarrassed or ashamed.

And it's clear that they still have love for their spouses.

They're just doing what's best for them.

Al grabbed my hand underneath the table.

I smiled at him, but internally, I was thinking about our marriage.

Al is as good of a guy as I'm going to get.

He's a much better guy than either of his friends.

So, why am I thinking about a divorce right now?

Al hasn't done anything wrong.

Divorcing him, for no reason, would kill him.

I just know it would.

Al is one of those guys who loves love.

He wants the type of love that his parents have. And he doesn't mind putting in the work to have it. Al will fix, change, adjust, revamp any and everything that he can to make me happy. He will do anything to make us work. I've seen him do it time and time again, with no questions asked. These days, it's me who isn't telling him what's going on inside my head. Al doesn't have a clue that something may be wrong.

I shook away my thoughts.

Al is enough.

He's more than enough.

I just have to shake off whatever this is I've been feeling lately. That's all I have to do.

I can do this.

I have to do this.

For the rest of dinner, I could tell that Al was bothered.

He smiled. He laughed. And he even cracked a few jokes, but he was definitely bothered.

After dinner, for the most part, our car ride home was in silence. But as soon as we pulled into our driveway, Al started to speak.

"I can't believe that's the last time we'll all be together like that. I can't believe they're all getting divorced."

"Yeah. It's shocking; especially Gia and Paul. They are the cutest couple I know. They always seemed so happy together. They always seemed so in love."

"I know," Al turned off the car. "I'm surprised that they're not fighting to make things work."

"Maybe they have. Maybe divorce is their last and final option."

I waited for Al as he got out of the car and walked around to the passenger side to open my door.

"Maybe."

We made it inside the house and headed up the stairs.

"All I know is that I would fight to the death of me to make my marriage work. I wouldn't just give up. You're too important to me to do that."

I kissed his lips just to ease his mind.

"I know you would," I smiled. "We're fine. And our friends, they're all going to be fine too."

Al followed me into the bathroom.

I could tell that he had more to say, but he didn't.

He simply undressed with me and joined me in the shower.

"I love you," he mumbled behind me.

"I love you, too."

And I do.

I really do.

It's just…

~***~

"Jump a little bit, Nema! Come on, get those pants over those hips," Sophie instructed as I started to hop. "All that good cooking you're doing for Al has your ass as big as a house!" Sophie attempted to help me. "Yes! There you go. Now, look in the mirror. Those pants look so damn good on you! Look at those hips, those thighs, and that ass!"

"Hype me up, owww! Hype me up!" I started to bounce around. Sophie didn't hesitate to join in.

I've always been a little on the thicker side, and I've always been shapely. I used to hate having such a big butt when I was younger, but as I got older, I realized that having a nice ass came with attention that I secretly and desperately needed.

"Now, come on, I need to get some pictures of you to put on my social media. Your ass is going to sell the hell out of this $300 outfit. Watch!"

I modeled the ivory and green outfit for Sophie as she snapped picture after picture.

"These pictures are perfect! Look how pretty you look, Nema!' Sophie showed me picture after picture.

Sophie always compliments me.

I used to think it was out of pity.

A blind man can see that I'm nowhere as pretty as she is, but over the years, her compliments started to feel less like pity and more like love.

"And you can have the outfit. Wear it somewhere nice; preferably around people with money so they can ask you where you got it from and you can send them my way," she laughed.

"Will do," I smiled at Sophie. "I like the way you've changed things around in here," I started to walk around the boutique. "It makes the place feel bigger."

"It does! And I love it!"

I watched Sophie as she tried on one of her new dresses. I have no idea how she still has the perfect body because she eats like a 475-pound man.

Sophie will eat her food, your food, and order food to-go. She's always been a hungry little bitch, but she never gains any weight. And she never diets.

Never.

I admired Sophie's physique as she twirled around in the mirror.

Standing next to Sophie, at times, was hard for me.

It was the absolute worse in our high school days.

Sophia is only a year younger than I am, which made her only a grade behind me.

In high school, I had eyes for this boy, Jerry Martinez. He was Hattian and Latino mixed.

Oh, God, he was so dreamy!

We flirted all ninth grade, and since my boobs had finally sprouted over the summer, I just knew Jerry was going to ask me to be his girlfriend the first day of tenth grade. And he probably would have....

If he hadn't laid eyes on Sophie.

Even in the ninth grade, Sophie's curves were in all the right places, and her beauty was undeniable.

Jerry smiled at me the first day of school, but when he noticed Sophie standing next to me, his mouth dropped open.

Literally.

He started to drool while staring at Sophie, and suddenly, I became invisible to him.

Needless to say, he started dating Sophie, and they were together all of six months before Sophie moved on to someone else.

That was only the beginning of living in the shadow of my little sister's beauty.

If a boy was talking to me, most likely, he was asking me about Sophie. Boys would offer me their lunch money and everything else in between, if I promised to help them get Sophie's attention.

Finally, at the end of the eleventh grade, a boy who transferred to our school, surprisingly took notice in me, instead of Sophie. Yet somehow, in the end, it all still led back to her.

Sophie ended up screwing him.

Granted, he and I were broken up when it happened.

His name was Erik and he dumped me because I wasn't ready to have sex. I wanted to be, but I couldn't force myself to be ready, and I couldn't force him to wait around until I was.

Sophie knew how heartbroken I was over the breakup. He was my first real boyfriend. He was the first boy to actually see my beauty and not my sister's.

Yet, my pain didn't stop Sophie from digging her horny little claws into him, only a year after our break-up.

I remember her simply asking me if it was okay to screw him before she did it. I was already dating someone else, and though she could've had any other guy, I guess she'd wanted my ex too.

But as I always say…

Sophie is just---Sophie.

You either hate her or you love her.

And I love my little sister.

I really do.

"Come take a selfie with me," Sophie said.

Despite all the attention, and the fact that I may not be as pretty as she is, I wouldn't say that I've ever been jealous of Sophie.

She wouldn't allow me to be.

Sophie has always been so loving towards me.

And our parents and Cam made sure we knew that we weren't each other's competition.

Mama always told us that we both shined in our own way. So, though it was hard, and sometimes I felt unseen, I was never jealous of Sophie's beauty. If anything, I was jealous of her personality, and how free-spirited she is.

I wish I had the balls to try, do or say some of the things that Sophie does. She does what she wants to do. Says what she wants to say. And she doesn't give a damn who likes it or not. Actually, she doesn't care if she's liked at all. Sophie doesn't have too many friends. Not because she can't make friends; everyone wants to be the pretty girl's friend. But Sophie actually prefers to have as few friends as possible. She will tell anyone that I'm her sister and her best friend. And that I'm the only friend that matters to her.

"So, did you ever screw that guy from the restaurant that night?" I asked Sophie after taking over twenty selfies with her.

"Oh, honey, yes. A complete waste of my time."

"Why? Was his dick little? His pants were a little tight. He couldn't have been packing too much dick inside them," I laughed.

"Oh, no, he was packing. His dick was long and thick. But he's too arrogant for me. Good dick is a plus. But more than anything, I want a sweet and gentle guy. I want a guy like Al. Only triple Al's salary," Sophie laughed.

I laughed because I knew she was serious.

Sophie meant exactly what she'd said.

"You're a girl who knows what she wants. I'll tell you that much."

"I just wish finding what I want was as easy as knowing. Dating in this day in time is stressful! These men lie, cheat, and tell you just about anything to get inside your pants. They call their wives their sisters. They think they should be rewarded with pussy if they pay for a dinner and a movie. And the wealthy ones are the worst! Women are no longer something of value to them. What one woman won't do...they'll just pay one that will. Girl, these men out here are something else! You better count your blessings. And be thankful that you have a good man to go home to."

We both turned our attention to the front door of the boutique.

"I'm sorry. We're closed!" Sophie yelled.

The man continued to wiggle the doorknob.

Sophie walked towards the door. "Vega? What do you want?" She stopped in front of the door and crossed her arms.

Vega? Who is Vega?

"Sophie, can we talk?" He screamed from the other side of the door.

"Nope." She turned away from the door.

"Please, Sophie! I love you!"

Sophie laughed and to my surprise, his comment made her turn around and open the door.

"You love me?" She asked him.

The man noticed me standing there just as he answered Sophie's question. "Yes. I do."

"Uh, Soph, I'm going to go," I grabbed my purse.

"Oh, no. You don't have to leave," she looked at me. "He's about to." She turned her attention back to Vega.

Heeeyy Vega!

I eyed the dark chocolate, tall, piece of a man wrapped in muscles, with long, neat dreadlocks.

Vega and Sophie actually make a really cute couple.

They would turn heads together, that's for sure.

"You don't love me," Sophie said to him. "And you want to know how I know this?" She asked, although she didn't have any plans on waiting for his answer. "Love is patient. Love is kind. Love is knowing whether I need a hug or a glass of wine. Love is loving someone else even on the days you don't love yourself. Love is choosing the same person every single day because for you, there's simply no one else. Love is being the first person you want to call whether you need to laugh or cry. Love is giving and giving and giving because no matter what happens, you never want to have to say goodbye. So, no, Vega. You don't love me. You may love how I look, or how I make you feel when I'm bouncing up and down your dick. You might even love how I rub the back of your head while you're in between my legs. But love, true love, perfect love…what you feel for me isn't even close."

And with that, Sophie pushed him out of her boutique and closed the door in his face.

She turned to me and with a smile she said: "Now, where were we?"

"Wow! Sophie, what you said about love was so beautiful! Is that really what love is to you?"

"Yes. And so much more," she stared at me. "What is love to you, Nema?"

I chuckled. "Good question."

~***~

"Remember when we got these tattoos? You were terrified," Al smiled as he played in my hair.

"I sure was. I thought it was going to hurt, but it didn't."

Al and I chose the infinity tattoos because at the time, it was the perfect tattoo for us. I truly did want to be with him forever, but these days, forever just seems so far away.

"It's time we get another one."

"I'll pass."

"What do you want to do for our anniversary this year?"

"I don't know. But if I know you like I think I do, I'm sure you probably already have something up your sleeve."

"Who me?" Al chuckled.

Along with the tattoos, Al took me on my first cruise for our first anniversary.

Al loves to travel.

He grew up taking family vacations a few times a year because Al's father is a retired scientist, and though they had a good bit of kids, they could afford it.

My parents worked hard for their money, and if they were able to take us to the beach just once a year, we were lucky.

Of course, after they were gone, I was in high school. And then, I went to college only a few hours away from home. Before Al, I'd only been on an airplane once.

He promised to show me the world, and he did just that every chance he could. One of the things that I love about Al is if he says it, he means it.

And a man who keeps his word is everything.

"Is it me or have you seemed a little tense lately?"

"I've been a little worried about not being able to draw or paint, that's all."

"Oh, baby, it'll come back to you."

"Yeah. That's what everyone keeps telling me," I forced a smile.

I glanced at the clock next to the bed, just before forcing myself out of Al's arms and standing to my feet. "You know what? You're on your own all weekend. I'm locking myself down in the basement and I'm not coming out until I draw something."

"Did you forget my parents will be here later today?"

"Damn it! I did. Is that why you were downstairs last night cleaning up like a housewife from the year 1957?"

"Yes. I'm surprised you forgot."

"Sorry. My mind has been all over the place lately."

"What can I do to help?"

"Nothing. I'll be fine," I kissed his hand. "Well, I'm going to head down and work for a little while anyway. Okay?"

I hurried downstairs to the basement before Al could ask me for anything, especially sex.

Al wants, needs, and prefers sex every single day.

Don't get me wrong, I love sex.

And two or three times a week is perfect for me.

But every single day…

These days, most days, I just don't want to!

I do it. I always have. Even when we were dating. If he wanted it, if he wanted me, I gave myself to him.

At first, it didn't bother me.

I did it, got it over with, and went on about my day. But for the past few months, I pray for days or nights that Al is too tired to want to touch me.

And those prayers aren't answered often.

Al almost refuses to go to sleep at night without having some kind of sex with me.

I guess I shouldn't be complaining.

Some men won't touch their wives for weeks and would rather go out and touch someone else.

And in this day in time, where women don't mind being the other woman, I'd better count my blessings.

And a good man like Al is a blessing.

I locked the basement door behind me in high hopes that the next few hours would be productive.

But before I got started, there was something else I wanted to do.

I made myself comfortable in a chair.

These days, fifty percent of the time when I have sex with Al I don't get anything from it. Most of the time I'm only having sex to please him. So, I pretend to cum so that he can hurry up and get his.

Now, sitting in the chair with my legs wide open, I pleased myself with a smile on my face.

For some strange reason, in that moment, I remembered that it was Lula who convinced me to touch myself for the first time.

Back in college, I caught her masturbating, and she didn't stop at the sight of me. She smiled and kept right on going. I rushed out of her dorm room, and she called me once she was done. She told me that if I didn't know what I like, how could I tell someone what to do to me?

I touched myself for the first time that same night.

"Whew!" I exhaled in satisfaction all of three minutes later.

I needed that.

Maybe a good orgasm will motivate me to create something great.

Wrong!

Two and a half hours, and just a random face sketch later, I was headed back up the basement stairs, to cook and get dressed before Al's parents arrived.

"Wow, I was just coming to cook," I examined the spread.

Al had fried chicken, baked macaroni and cheese, asparagus and cheddar biscuits already on the table.

"I got this," he smiled.

"How did I get so lucky?"

Al walked over and kissed my lips. "Nah, I'm the lucky one," he said. "Now, go and get dressed."

I did as I was told.

Al's parents are perfect; hence why he's such a good guy. He has a loving mother, a hardworking father, and his parents have been married for over forty years.

Al looks up to them, more than anyone, and in a way, I look up to them too. More so in the beginning.

I used to call his mom "Superwoman" because of the many roles she had to play to so many people. I used to think that I would be just like her someday, but I'm sad to say that right now, trying to be superwoman is growing less and less appealing to me.

The doorbell chimed just as I finished getting dressed.

"There she is!" My mother-in-law greeted me as I came down the stairs. "Hey, darling, how have you been? Muuah!" She planted a big wet kiss on my cheek.

"I'm doing good."

"And you look good, too!" Al's mother, Teresa, complimented me. I hugged Al's dad, Alfonzo Sr. and we all headed into the kitchen.

"Those baby making hips seem to have spread. Is there something the two of you need to tell me?" Teresa smiled as she took her seat.

"Oh, no ma'am, not yet. And not anytime soon," I replied.

"What do you mean not anytime soon?" Al asked. "I plan on putting a baby in you by the end of this year."

I looked at him confused. "Uh, says who? I don't remember having this discussion," I forced a smile.

"What is there to discuss? We both want kids."

"Yes, but when the time is right."

"We've been married for almost two years. And together for five. We've had our time. Now, it's baby making time," Al wore a huge smile.

I tried my best to keep a smile plastered on my face.

I'm not ready for kids.

Initially, yes, I thought I would be by now, but I'm not exactly where I want to be in life, in my career, or with my goals. I turned thirty in January, and other than having a husband, I don't feel like I've accomplished much else.

"Maybe we should change the subject," Al's mother chimed it. "This seems as though it should be more of a private conversation."

Al shrugged. I simply nodded.

"So, what's been going on you two? Tell me everything!"

Dinner went well and once Al's parents were comfortable in our guest bedroom, Al and I headed into our room.

"Al?" I said as soon as the door was closed. "I'm not ready to have a baby."

"Really? I thought we agreed to start trying year two of our marriage."

"I know. That was the plan. I just feel like I have so much more to accomplish first. There's so much more I want to do; especially career-wise."

"Honestly, when we start a family, you can stay home with the baby, and just focus on your art. You know I'll take care of you."

"Yes, but I don't think I would want to just stay home. And maybe I would if I could actually work on my art, but who knows, maybe I've lost my touch. It's just…"

Al kissed me. "We're going to be fine. And when we have a baby, everything will be fine then too."

Al comes from a big family, and a family who is very family-oriented. I've always known how badly he wants kids, and that he wants as many as I'll give him. And I know what we planned but…

Plans change.

Things change.

Everything…

Everything is changing.

~***~

"You said he was getting a divorce, right?" Sophie asked about Al's friend, Jack.

"Yes, but no Sophie. Stay away."

"Why? You know I've always had my eye on his sexy ass."

Jack is pretty sexy.

His father is Cuban, and his mother is mixed with Black and White.

Jack has short curly hair, big brown eyes, a nice smile, average height, and a smoking hot body! He goes to the gym three or four days a week, and it shows!

Their friend Paul is pretty attractive too. If you ask me, Paul and Al look as though they could be brothers.

"The man isn't even divorced yet, and you're already plotting on him."

Sophie shrugged. "As soon as the ink is dry, I'm shooting my shot!"

"Please. Don't. And thank you," I rolled my eyes with a smile.

Sophie and I are getting pedicures together, which has sort of become a monthly routine.

"I'm just kidding. He doesn't make enough money to maintain a woman like me."

"Soph, you make your own money."

"So! It's a man's job to provide."

Well, I can't argue with that.

"I'll fuck him, though. Give him my number."

"Never."

"Fine. I'll give it to him myself," Sophie laughed.

I exhaled loudly as I glanced down at my cell phone.

"What?" Sophie asked.

"Al keeps sending me baby names."

"Oh, my god! Are you pregnant?"

"No."

"Oh," Sophie relaxed.

"But Al is ready to start trying and I'm not."

"Well, just tell him that."

"I tried. He's trying to change my mind."

Sophie spoke softly to the lady painting her toenails, and then she looked over at me in amusement. "Nema, why are you being so damn difficult? Just have the man's babies! Shoot, have as many as you can by him. You're not getting any younger. Before long, those titties will sag, and that ass will start to drag. Go on and pop out a baby or two while you're still cute," Sophie giggled. "Seriously, though, you guys are going to make great parents."

"Soph..." I hesitated. "Lately...lately I just feel..."

"What?"

"Nevermind."

I decided that Sophie wasn't the best person to talk to about what I've been feeling lately. And it isn't because she's not married. Sophie just sees everything so…uncomplicated, I should say. She acts as if there's a simple solution to everything. And maybe to her, and for her, there is.

Once Sophie and I were done at the nail salon, I called Gia, Paul's wife, well, soon to be ex-wife.

She agreed to meet me for lunch.

"Hey, girlie," Gia greeted me a few minutes later at the restaurant. "How are you?"

"I'm okay. And you? Especially after that bomb y'all dropped on us."

Gia laughed. "Girl, I hate to say it like this but…I'm better than ever! Like, I'm so happy that it's almost over!"

"Really?"

"Really. You know, sometimes, love just don't stick. Sometimes love just isn't enough. And we accepted that. Our divorce will be final, soon, and I'm just ready for the next chapter in my life, you know?"

Gia and Paul have been married for about five or six years. On the surface, you would've never guessed that they were unhappy or that they were having problems. But then again, I guess that's how it's supposed to be.

"Gia…"

I knew our conversation would stay between us, but I knew once I said my next sentence, there was no taking it back.

"Gia…I feel…trapped. I feel…I think I feel unhappy."

Gia's eyes widened. "With Al? Nooooo! Al isn't like my husband, or anyone else's husband. Al is a saint!"

"That he is. And maybe that's just it. Maybe he's just too perfect, which makes me want to be perfect. And trying to be the perfect wife causes me to neglect everything else that's important to me," I frowned. "I just feel like I'm not flourishing, at least not the way I want to be. I can't even do the one thing I love, which is create, because I feel so uninspired lately. When we got married, Al became my number one priority. And I thought I was okay with that. But the truth is, now, I'm not. It's like…I don't know. It's like, sometimes, I feel like my marriage is in my way. In a way, I feel like I just want to be free. And I'm starting to feel that way every single day."

Gia didn't respond.

"I know I have an amazing husband. I know that. Everyone knows that. But I can't give him what he wants right now. Well, it's more like I don't want to."

"Well, just tell him that."

"I tried. He wants to start working on trying to have a baby. I told him that I'm not ready. He's not listening. All I want is to operate in my gift, and start making a living doing the thing that I love, but I can't even do that. I know, I sound crazy."

"No, you're entitled to feel whatever it is that you're feeling. That's something that I had to learn. Your feelings are valid. Your feelings are yours."

"I just don't want to hurt him. He's such a good person. And he has been so good to me. Maybe it's just me. Maybe I'm going through something. I don't know."

Gia touched my hand. "I'm going to tell you something that someone once told me. Space brings clarity. As hard as it may be, ask Al for some time and space. See how you feel then. See if anything changes. For us, the space changed nothing and we both knew it was time to let go and walk away. For you, maybe some space will change everything. In a good way."

I nodded my head.

Gia is right.

Maybe I just need a few days to myself or a few weeks to clear my head and sort out my thoughts and feelings. A few days where I don't have to worry about anyone but myself. A few days where I don't have to cook, clean, or have sex when I'm tired.

Yes.

Some time and space to myself may be just what I need. The problem is Al and getting him onboard.

I know for a fact he's not going to want to be away from me.

I finished lunch with Gia, and I headed to the park.

Though Savannah is known for Forsyth Park, Emmet Park is my favorite.

Al's too.

I go there often. Most of the time just to sit and think.

"Ma'am, can I sit here?" A man asked after I'd been sitting on a bench at the park for about twenty minutes.

"Sure."

The man took a seat.

I tried not to stare at him, but it was hard not to.

He was so attractive, with magical, somewhat lime green eyes.

His skin was the same color as butter scotch, and I wondered what kind of cologne he was wearing.

He smells so good.

"Long day?" He asked.

"Not really. I just like to come here to clear my head."

"Me too. I come here in between appointments."

"Appointments?" I stared at his suit. "Let me guess, you're a lawyer. Or maybe you're in real estate."

He chuckled. "Nah. I sell dick."

I choked.

"Excuse me?"

"I'm an escort. Gigolo. Sex therapist. Cock slinger. Whatever you want to call me."

I couldn't do anything but laugh.

I laughed so hard that he started to laugh too.

"There's no shame in my game. You gotta' use your good-looks and special talents in any way you can these days. And my talents are needed…often. You'd be surprised how many women pay for a good time and good dick." He paused. "Are you looking for either?"

"Oh, no, I'm married."

"Shit, married women are my best customers. About seventy-five percent of the women I sleep with are married."

"Wow. Really? Then again, I'm not surprised."

"Husbands are lazy. I pick up the slack."

"Apparently, you do."

"Your man must be treating you right."

"He does. He's a great guy."

He stared at me. "Yeah, he may be great…but you're not happy. I can see it in your eyes. And if there's one thing that I know, it's an unhappy woman."

"Yeah, but my unhappiness has nothing to do with him. It's in regard to me, and my "special talent", as you said. I really do have a good husband."

He stood up.

"Good for who?" The gentleman tugged on his tie, and without saying another word, he started to strut away.

Damn!

Look at that walk.

Good Dick Draco used to walk like that.

I couldn't help but to wonder how much he charges for sex. I should've asked him.

I watched him until he was out of sight.

His comment "good for who" rang in my ears.

Why isn't Al good enough for me anymore?

"Baby!" Al screamed later on that evening as he walked in from work. He paused at the sight of my bags and a mountain full of my art supplies on the floor by the door. "Nema, what's this?"

"Al, baby, sit down."

After talking to Gia and the man at the park, I realized that space really is what's best for me right now.

I need to get my thoughts and feelings together.

And I can't do that around Al.

"I don't want to sit down," he stared at my bags. "Baby, what is this? Wait, are you leaving me?"

"No, well, not in the way that you're probably thinking."

Al looked confused.

"Look, lately, I've been having these feelings…"

"What feelings?"

"If you hush, I can tell you."

Al exhaled.

"It's like I've felt stuck. I've felt like I'm not where I'm supposed to be in my life. And it's not you. It's me. I feel like I've put so much into my marriage these past two years, so much so that I neglected everything else that was important to me. And now I regret it."

"What are you talking about? I've never asked you to give up anything, Nema."

"I know. I just felt it was my duty to lay off of certain things to make sure you were my top priority. Now, I just feel…" I took a deep breath. "I just feel like I need a little space. I need some clarity. With all the baby talk, and with me not feeling inspired and not being able to do the one thing I really want to do…" I exhaled. "I just need a little time."

"Time?" Al huffed. "Time away from me? Away from our marriage? So, you don't want us anymore?"

I could see the hurt all over his face.

"I never said that. I love you. I love us. You are literally the best husband ever. I swear you are. So, don't think for a second that this is about you. It isn't. Not at all. This is about me. I figured I would just stay over at Sophie's for a week or two and just see if I can sort through whatever this is that I'm feeling. I just woke up one day and I was feeling unaccomplished. I was feeling stagnant. I was feeling different."

Al looked as though he wanted to cry.

Or yell.

I couldn't really tell.

"I'll go. You can stay," finally, my husband mumbled.

"No. This is my issue. I'm not running you out of our house."

"It's fine," Al walked past me. "All of this is about painting and doing the one thing you love, right? Well, you'll need your studio. You don't want to be around me. I'll go. You stay."

"Al, that's not what I said."

He didn't respond.

For the next hour, I watched Al carry a few of his things to the car. He didn't say a word until he was finally ready to leave.

"I'll never give up on us, Nema. And I won't let you give up on us either." Al kissed my lips. "I love you. I'll call you when I get to Jack's."

And with that, my husband was gone.

****

THREE

"Damn, who died?"

I laughed at Sophie's question.

"Nobody. Al keeps sending me flowers."

Al has been staying at his friend Jack's house for about a week. He has been attempting to give me space.

Emphasis on the word attempting.

Al hasn't been back to the house since the day he left, but he has sent dozens of flowers with beautiful notes attached to them.

Every single day.

"I know that's right! Fight for your woman, Al!" Sophie smelled the bouquet of white roses on the coffee table. "I don't know why you're doing him like this. That's a damn good man! And your crazy ass don't even want him!" My sister rolled her eyes. "You're going to lose him if you don't get your shit together."

"I'm trying."

Needless to say, in a week of space, nothing has changed.

Even without a husband to tend to, I still haven't been able to paint anything new. I've been coming home from work, every day, and sitting down in the basement for hours, doing absolutely nothing.

"It's hard out here in these "Single Streets". Trust me. You don't want these problems."

"Maybe they aren't problems. Freedom isn't a bad problem to have."

"Is that what you're missing? Your freedom?"

"Maybe. In a way," I shrugged. "I've been so focused on making sure I keep Al happy for these past few years that I ended up feeling unhappy. Now, I'm just searching for my own personal happiness again. That's all."

"Well, don't take too long. I don't care how good of a man he is…no one waits forever."

For the first time, Sophie noticed what I was wearing.

"Uh, where are you going looking like that?"

"It's Vanessa's, my friend from work, birthday. She's having a little something to celebrate. Normally, I wouldn't go because Al works so hard during the week and on Friday nights he likes for us to do something together, but since he's not here, I'm going."

Sophie looked down at her clothes.

"Can I go? I mean I'm basically dressed for a night out anyway."

Sophie is always dressed to impress.

One of the perks of owning your own boutique, I guess.

Sophie was wearing a fitted purple strapless dress, gold open toed heels, and gold accessories.

"Yeah. Come on. You can go."

We arrived at the K-Lavish Lounge and Nightclub, about ten minutes late because Sophie took forever to decide what she wanted to do with her hair. In the end, she ended up wearing it exactly how it had been from the very beginning.

"Oh, somebody pinch me because I must be dreaming!" Vanessa squealed. "You came! I didn't expect you to come! My married friends never come!"

Her comment made me feel bad.

She does invite me out, all the time, and I always say no because of Al.

He loves quality time and he's always so full of surprises that I was always worried about making night-time plans with someone else, not knowing if he had something up his sleeve.

Though Vanessa and I are pretty close, I haven't told her about the whole space thing with Al. I guess I'm just not sure if there's really anything to tell yet.

"I hope it's okay that I brought my sister." It wasn't until then that I noticed that Sophie wasn't standing beside me anymore. Briefly, I scanned the crowd until I spotted her dress. "Well, I brought my sister. But as you can see, she will most likely be doing her own thing."

Vanessa smiled just before yelling, "Who wants shots?" towards the ladies behind her. "Let's get this party started!"

At first, I tried to take things slow.

It's been a long time since I've been out at a club and I somewhat felt uncomfortable in the beginning. But after a few shots too many, I found myself having the time of my life.

I ended up on the dance floor, dancing as though I've never danced before.

"Go, Nema! Go, Nema! Go, Nema!"

Vanessa and her crew cheered me on.

And full of liquor courage, I started to shake, pop, drop and I even tried to do a split like I used to back in the day.

Can someone say: A huge fucking mistake!

Once I was down, I couldn't get back up.

Literally.

"No, Nema! No, Nema! No, Nema!" The crowd started to chant.

"Nema, get your stupid ass up off that floor!" I heard Sophie say in a deep whisper inside my ear.

"I would if I could. Help Me!"

It took a minute or two, but Sophie managed to help me to my feet.

"Party girl has had enough for the night," Sophie said to Vanessa. "Come on, let's get you home."

"No! I don't want to go home!"

"Too bad! You're going!"

Sophie had to practically drag me out of the building.

"I had so much fun!" I sang. "I haven't had that much fun in years!

"Nema, get your drunk ass in the car!"

"Hey, you're not the boss of me," I squeezed Sophie's nose as she pulled the seat belt across my chest.

Sophie giggled. "You are so drunk."

"And it feels so good!"

Al doesn't drink. He may have a glass of wine every now and then, or have one drink socially, but I've never seen him drunk. And because I didn't want to look crazy or like a drunk in front of him, I only have wine, every now and then, and never over two glasses.

I realized that though he's never actually asked me to change certain things about myself, I did them because I wanted to make sure he approved of me.

"I don't want to be perfect anymore, Sophie," I mumbled.

Sophie stopped at a red light. "Then, don't be."

"But what if my husband doesn't love me anymore if I'm not?"

Sophie didn't respond.

"You were right, Sophie. Al is the perfect guy. But you know what?" I slurred. "Just because he's perfect, that doesn't mean that he's perfect for me." I managed to say before I puked all over myself.

Sophie started to fuss at me and ordered me to roll down the window.

"You have such an exciting life," I yelled as the wind slapped my face.

"But I would trade lives with you in a heartbeat," Sophie exhaled. "I really would."

"Be careful what you wish for," I said. "Because sometimes, a wish that comes true could very well become a wish you never should've made in the first place."

~***~

"I heard somebody had a good time Friday night," Diana laughed at me as soon as I walked into work Monday morning. "I hate I missed it. I would've loved seeing Little Miss Perfect let her hair down."

"Good morning to you too, Diana."

Diana rolled her eyes as she walked away.

"Ugh, why does she always have a nasty ass attitude?" Vanessa approached me in all smiles.

"She only acts that way with you," she chuckled. "But hey, there Ms. Life of the Party. How are you feeling?"

"Better. Finally. I felt like crap the entire weekend. My legs are still sore."

"They should be. All that popping and dropping you were doing, chica! I thought you were going to hurt yourself!"

"And I did." I frowned. "I'm never going out with you again."

"Aw, don't be like that!" Vanessa laughed.

"I love your hair like this by the way," I touched her new short bob haircut.

Vanessa is Latina, and to go with her big breasts, and big natural booty, she always wore big, natural curly hair.

"Thank you! I'm trying something new. Maybe my new hair will get me a new man."

"And hopefully your big personality doesn't scare him away!"

"Nema?"

Both Vanessa and I looked behind me at the sound of her voice.

Lula.

My college classmate.

Vanessa walked away as Lula came closer to me.

"Hi, Lula. What brings you by? Was something wrong with your purchase?"

"Oh. No. That painting is worth every brown penny I spent on it," she smiled. "Actually, that's why I'm here."

Lula followed me over to our lounging area.

"Remember the "Paint Me Blue" project we had in college?"

"Oh, my gosh! How can I forget it? The college still has my piece on display."

"Does your work still have a similar style? I'm on the hunt for about three new pieces, but in that particular style. I want to use them in the entertaining space of my new home. Do you have anything similar completed? Just name your price. And don't be scared now, I have plenty of money to spend!" Lula laughed. "Oh, and I may have bragged on you just a little to a few of the ladies in my circle. And just so happens, one of them is opening a new gynecologist office, and she said if you're as good as I say you are, she may want you to do some custom work for her entire office."

I started to sweat.

These are the type of opportunities that I've longed for.

My work being seen and admired by hundreds, or even thousands of people.

"Nema?"

I cleared my throat. "I, uh, don't have anything similar to the college project, but maybe I can work my magic..."

"Yes! Yes! Yes! Oh, my, thank you!" Lula interrupted me. "Okay, how about this: I'm having a Pearls and Girls Brunch gathering next month, do you think you could have something done by then? Oooh, actually, the gynecologist friend that I was just telling you about will be there too. So, maybe you can bring a few options and we can sort of have our own little private auction. I'll get first dibs, though. The other ladies can go at it for whatever you have left. They're all wealthy, so, I assume just like here, the highest bid will win!" Lula stood up. "I gave you my card last time I was here. Use it. If you finish with something you think I'll like before the brunch, reach out to me. I would love to already have a painting or two on my walls before the guests arrive. I want something bold, feminine…and sexy! Hell, I want to make those rich bitches jealous!" Lula snickered.

"Lula, I don't know what to say. Thank you."

"No thanks needed. Besides, if memory serves me correctly, I passed a few of those classes because of you." Lula put on her Dolce and Gabbana sunglasses. "When you get a chance, contact me and I'll give you the brunch details. I look forward to seeing what you come up with! Ciao!"

Lula is a millionaire.

My work could be purchased by a millionaire!

And it could be seen by other millionaires.

Hell, if I think bigger…my work could make *me* a millionaire!

There's just one problem…

Me.

This is a golden opportunity and most likely one that I'm going to miss out on if I can't get my shit together!

There has to be a way to get my spark back.

"What was that all about?" Diana asked.

"Nothing. She just had some comments on her painting."

Diana looked as though she wanted to say something else, but she didn't.

Good.

I don't have time for her smart as mouth today, anyway. I have much more important things on my mind.

I could barely focus on work the entire day from thinking about Lula and her brunch.

As soon as I clocked out, I drove like a bat out of hell, all the way home, eager to get to the basement.

To my surprise, Al was waiting for me when I got there.

"Al."

"Nema," he embraced me.

"Is everything okay?"

"Yes. Everything is fine. I'm coming home."

"Al..."

"I know you said you need space, and I gave you space. If you don't want to have kids now or ever, we don't have to. I'll compromise. I just want you. I just want my wife."

"Al, we said we were going to talk about this before you came back home."

"I know. I just can't spend another day away from you. It's driving me crazy, baby. I swear, I just want to be here with you. I love you."

I'm not ready.

I thought the words, but I didn't say them.

Instead, I allowed Al to hug me as tight as he could.

This is why I should've left and stayed at Sophie's.

In the back of my mind, I knew that when Al was ready to come back home, he was coming, whether I was ready for him to or not.

Unfortunately, I didn't make it to the basement until three hours later. And before I even sat down, I knew that I wouldn't get anything done.

I came home full of excitement and energy. But after a long conversation with Al, dinner, and intense make-up sex, I didn't have anything left to give.

Beyond frustrated, I frowned.

Al coming back home, now, is only going to make things worse between us.

I can feel it.

I took a seat on the off-gray futon in the corner of the basement. Before long, I found myself stretched out, underneath a blanket, looking at pictures of my college painting that Lula referenced.

Paint Me Blue.

It really is an amazing work of art.

I tried to channel where I was at that time in my life.

I was a junior in college.

I was single. And if memory serves me correctly, I hadn't had sex in about three months at the time.

Oh, and I'd spent my entire spring break down on our Aunt Taleda's farm.

Aunt Taleda is our mother's oldest sister.

She was prepared to take Sophie and I in if Cam hadn't chosen to keep us.

Thank God, he did.

Though, I'd had a ball chasing chickens, milking cows, riding horses and all the experiences of life on a farm; I most certainly wouldn't want to live on one.

Anyway, I remember we were given the art assignment before we went on spring break, and it was due as soon as we got back. At the farm, I remember taking all of my utensils outside one night, one by one.

And after setting up my art easel and my portable table, with nothing but the moonlight, animal noises, and the dozens of night lights surrounding the farm, I started to paint.

I remember not really being able to see the colors on the paper, but I continued to paint anyway.

The background of the painting had shades of yellow, black and red. And somehow, I tied in a woman's face covered in strokes of blue; many, many shades of blue, brown and a touch of gray. The finished product somewhat resembled a face where fury and serenity manage to intertwine. Remembering that night, as accurately as possible; I remember feeling a bit overwhelmed by nature, the animals and everything that farm life had to offer.

I was at peace.

I felt free.

I had no idea that my painting was going to be such a hit, but it was. My art professor raved on and on about my painting and even convinced me to enter it into a few contests. I ended up winning second place in one of them along with a $500 cash prize.

I allowed the school to keep the painting.

I figured that one day, I would create new ones that would be even better.

Maybe I should go visit my aunt's farm.

And I would prefer to go without Al, though I know that most likely, he'll insist on coming with me.

But visiting the farm is worth a try.

The brunch is a month away.

And by then, I'm determined to have created something magical!

Something memorable.

Something extraordinary!

And who am I kidding?

Something that's going to make me rich!

Hopefully.

~***~

"Sophie, that's like the fifth guy you've called in less than ten minutes."

"I know. I'm trying to decide what type of dick I'm in the mood for."

"What?"

"Look, I'm looking for love. But until I find the right one...a girl has options. Lots of them!" She laughed. "Too many. I'm forgetting which dick belongs to who. I think I'm in the mood for "Nut or Die" sex," Sophie smacked her lips.

"What the hell is "Nut or Die" sex."

"Well, the guy chokes you harder and harder until he gets his nut. So, your pussy better do what it's supposed to do, otherwise, the man on top of you better know how to do CPR! That's all I can say!" Sophie was amused. "Teddy? Yep. I'm in the mood for Teddy."

Flabbergasted, I watched Sophie start to text away.

Maybe some strange type of sex is what Al and I need.

He's been walking around on eggshells since he's been home. He isn't saying much of anything unless I say something to him, and I can tell that he's trying to make sure he doesn't do anything that could potentially lead to me asking him to leave.

He still doesn't get it.

It really is me and not him.

He hasn't asked for sex since the first day coming back, which is new.

I'm sure he wants it, but the fact that he's trying not to require the usual from me, just shows how much he really does care about me and whatever this is that I'm going through.

Sophie finished setting up her dick appointment, said a few more words to me, and then she said her goodbyes.

I watched Sophie walk until she was out of sight.

The auction house is only two blocks away from Sophie's boutique. It was her turn to come to my job to have lunch and she'd decided to walk instead of drive.

I stood next to the entrance of the auction house as I texted Al. I pretended to be horny as I told him to come straight home from work and to beep his car horn once he was outside.

Al and I have never had car sex.

Maybe an exciting, sexual encounter will be good for both of us. Hopefully, in more ways than one.

"Ahhh!"

I jumped.

Diana had been standing right behind me, as quiet as a mouse.

"Why are you just standing there like a crazy person?"

Diana didn't respond.

She simply headed back inside the auction house without saying a word.

I'm convinced that she's some kind of nutcase.

In that moment, I realized how little I actually know about her. She's been around for almost a year, but Diana never talks about anyone or anything from her personal life. Hell, she never talks about anything personal at all.

Either she's talking about work, complaining, or insulting someone.

That's pretty much it.

I worked hard for the rest of the day with thoughts of Al, Lula and painting on my mind.

I was full of anxiety and desperation.

I haven't felt this anxious about anything, in a long time. Not since I thought I was pregnant the first year after I graduated college.

I was sleeping with two different men, at the same time. I wasn't in a relationship with either of them. And usually, I would only have unprotected sex with one of them. But one day, I slept with both of them, hours apart, without a condom.

Not my proudest moment.

But it happened.

And it is what it is.

Men do it all the time.

Anyway, my period was late that month, and I thought I was going to massive heart attack waiting for it to show up. I took two or three pregnancy tests, every day, for two weeks straight. I could barely sleep from going to the bathroom to check for just a speck of blood. I'd convinced myself that I was pregnant, and even started having fake symptoms, but finally, my period showed up and I promised to never put myself in that situation again.

"Oh, my God!"

Al growled, full of lust and excitement.

I'd rushed home from work to shower, and now, I'm having car sex with my husband.

It's six o'clock in the evening, still sunny, yet inside his car in our driveway, I bounced up and down on his dick like a pogo stick.

"Ooooh," I moaned.

I felt such a rush!

As I bounced up and down, faster and faster, my moans grew louder and louder.

"Yes, baby, yes," Al said underneath me.

I was so consumed with excitement that I almost forgot he was there.

"Oh, baby, I'm about to cum!" I screamed.

"Come on, then baby. Cum for me."

And I did.

I erupted like a volcano all over Al's dick.

"Wow," Al exhaled. "Just…wow."

After ensuring that my dress was down over my bare ass, I opened the car door and practically crawled out of it.

It wasn't until then that I noticed our neighbors Todd and April standing in their front yard with their mouths hanging wide open.

I laughed as I waved at them.

They both grinned back as though they'd enjoyed the show.

"Well, it looks like we had an audience," Al finally got out of the car and joined me at my side.

"Are you embarrassed?" I asked him.

"Hell no! We can go at it again if you want to."

I shook my head no, as I attempted to walk out the cramp in my left leg. "No. I'm good. I needed that. And now, I'm going to get to work."

"I'll clean up and then go out and get dinner."

Al showered, and as soon as he walked out the door to go and get food, I washed up and then, I headed down to the basement.

Needless to say, all I managed to paint was some weird sort of vagina-flower combo.

Surely nothing worth showing to a single soul.

Damn it!

If hot, sweaty, spontaneous sex can't get the job done, then I don't know what will!

~***~

"I can't believe you went to visit Aunt Taleda," Cam shook his head. "I hate that farm. A horse tried to rape me on that farm."

Sophie howled in laughter. "Say what?"

"I kid you not! That horse was after me. No one believed me. But it chased my ass around that farm like I was fresh meat!"

I let out a chuckle. "It still looks the same. And Aunt Taleda is still hell on wheels! That lady still moves around like a twenty-year-old. She'll probably out live all of us."

The waiter placed our pizzas on the table.

"The trip was a waste of time though. I was hoping that being down there would help me get into the zone, but it didn't."

"How did Al like being down there?"

"Girl, he got fucked up so many times," I laughed. "The chickens chased him. The hogs tried to eat him. And one of the horses took a shit on his shoe."

"Oh, my god!" Sophie laughed so loud that people started to look at our table.

"That's hilarious," Cam said.

"He tried his best to be a farm boy. He wanted to help do everything. Now, he's home all bruised up and exhausted."

Since coming back from the farm, Al has been needy, and I've been extremely annoyed.

He begged to come with me, just like I knew he would, but now, my free time is being spent catering to him, instead of on what really matters to me the most, at the moment.

"Are y'all good?" Sophie asked.

"I was just about to ask the same thing," Cam looked at me.

"Honestly, I don't think so. I asked for space. I don't feel like it was long enough to really figure everything out."

"How long do you need, Nema?"

"I don't know. But I know that Al coming back home, before I could figure out what's going on with me, just made everything worse," I frowned.

I hate feeling this way about Al and my marriage, but it's the truth.

"So, what are you saying?" Cam asked.

I thought carefully about my next words.

"What are you trying to say, Nema?"

"I'm saying…maybe marriage isn't for me anymore. At least not right now. I'm saying…I think I'm saying that I'm going to ask Al for a divorce."

Sophie started to talk a mile per minute.

Cam didn't say a thing.

"He deserves someone who can be all in. And I can't give him that right now. Not anymore. I need real space. And I can't ask him to put his life on hold for me while I figure my shit out."

"So, when are you going to tell him?"

"Soon. I'll probably come and stay with you Sophie, until I can find a place."

"You know you'll always be welcomed at my house, anytime. You don't ever have to ask for a place to stay. I just say really think about this before you do it."

I glanced at my brother. "Cam?"

"What?"

"Do you have anything to say?"

"Nope."

Cam took a bite of his pizza and simply continued to listen as Sophie and I went back and forth.

Cam and Al have become quite close over the years.

I can only assume that he just wants to stay out of it.

"Is it really that bad?"

"I didn't say it was bad. I'm just saying that right now, I want something else. I want more, for myself. And what I want for myself doesn't have a thing to do with Al. It's hard for me to explain."

"You don't have to explain," Cam finally spoke. "It's your marriage. It's your choice. It's your life. Do what's best for you. As long as you're happy, that's all that matters to me."

"Cam is only saying what he thinks he's supposed to say," Sophie blurted out. "I'm saying what you need to hear. And if you leave Al, you'll be a goddamn fool! And I mean, a big fat, fucking fool!" Sophie rolled her eyes.

"You're going to regret it. Mark my words. Take a damn trip! Get a tattoo! Smoke some crack! No, please don't do that. But if you're missing excitement, hell, go out and have one-night stand. And for the love of God, quit the damn job that reminds you every single day that someone else is out there doing the one thing that you love and can't seem to do right now!" Sophie yelled at me. "Do whatever you have to do to get out of this funk. But I'm telling you, don't divorce that man."

Sophie picked up a slice of pizza.

"And I'm telling you, if I do divorce my husband...he's off limits! Do you understand me?"

I have to spell the shit out for Sophie because she does have the tendency to disrespect a boundary or two.

"Really, Nema? I would never! You really think I would go behind you with Al?"

"I just had to put it out there. It wouldn't be the first time you've been with one of my exes."

"But I asked you."

"See. The fact that you think that makes it okay is why I said what I said."

Sophie stared at me as though she wanted to say something else, but she didn't.

Cam suggested that we change the subject.

We didn't talk about my marriage for the remainder of the time I was there. Just as we decided to get ice cream, Al sent me a text message asking me to come home right away.

"Y'all, I gotta' go." I flashed the front of my phone towards them. "Duty...I mean, Al, calls...again."

"See, that's the problem. You're looking at your marriage as a duty." Sophie was clearly unhappy with the whole possibly-getting-a-divorce thing.

"Duty. Responsibility. Obligation. It's all the same thing. And no matter what you call it, I don't want it anymore, Sophie. I just don't want it anymore."

I rushed home just in case something really was wrong with Al. He greeted me at the front door, smiling and perfectly fine.

"What's wrong? Is everything okay?"

Al grinned. "Yes." He grabbed my hand and started to lead me towards the kitchen.

"Al, where are we going?"

"We're going back to Paris, baby!"

"What?"

Al stopped in front of the basement door.

I could tell that he was still in pain by the way he rubbed his outer thigh, but he tried to focus on the matter at hand.

"Go on."

Somewhat agitated, I headed down the basement stairs.

"Oh, Al!"

Al had turned our basement into…

Paris!

There were beautiful lights, enlarged photos of all the beautiful places we visited while in Paris, French macaroons, and to top it off, there was a statue that looked identical to the Eiffel Tower sitting in the corner of the basement dazzled in warm, shinning, blush-colored lights.

"Al…I…"

"What better way to find your inspiration again than in your favorite place in the entire world?" Al smiled at me. "So, I brought Paris to you. And for the next few days, I'm going to bring you everything you need. Your favorite French dishes from that restaurant on Peach Avenue that you love. Look," Al said. "I packed you a bag. You can use the shower down here, and I packed the small fridge with your favorite snacks, water and wine. You literally don't have to leave this basement for the next few days. I won't bother you. All you have to do is stay down here and create." Al snapped his fingers. "Oh, I also spoke to Vanessa two days ago, who officially put you in as on vacation for the next three days, starting today. You don't have to be back at work until Monday. So, you have three days, plus the weekend to do what you do best."

When I couldn't find the words, I started to whine.

"Don't cry, baby. Don't cry."

"You really did all of this? Just to help me get my muse back?"

Well, now I feel like shit for the things I've been saying and feeling about him lately.

"I'll do anything for you," Al answered. "And I do mean anything. I wanted to whisk you away to Paris, but I can't get out of a work meeting, so, I had to get creative."

I beamed at him.

Every thought, every feeling, and every word I've said about divorcing Al was suddenly, instantaneously, forgotten.

I love my husband.

And you know what, I think I'll keep him!

~***~

"Uhhh…what is it?" Al eyed my painting.

"I have no idea."

It's day two in Paris-themed basement, and all I can say is…at least I've painted something.

"Uh, I think you should try again," Al said as he kissed my forehead.

"So, you think it's ugly?"

"Well, it's something," he said making his way back up the basement stairs. As soon as he closed the door, I exhaled.

Al is right…

The painting is hideous!

I took a whiff of the mouthwatering quiche that Al had left on the table beside me.

Al is keeping his word.

He hasn't bothered me one bit.

He hasn't even called me and the only time I've seen him is when he comes down to bring me food.

Nothing is stopping me.

No one is bothering me.

Nothing is in my way.

And still…

I devoured my food, and with a blank canvas in front of me, I thought about Paris.

I'd dreamt about going to Paris since I was ten years old. I used to talk about it all the time with my parents and siblings.

I would try to imagine what it was going to be like, but I'm proud to say that my imagination fell short.

Paris was so much more!

It was so romantic.

I had no idea Al was going to take me there to propose.

I remember the knee-length white dress I was wearing and the red flower in my hair. I remember holding Al's sweaty hand. And then, I remember him getting down on one knee right in front of the Eiffel Tower to ask me to be his wife.

Best proposal ever!

I smiled.

And then…

I picked up the paintbrush and focused on my memories.

A stroke here.

A stroke there.

Red.

Brown.

Blue.

Green.

Yes. It needs a little green.

I became lost in the colors and by the time I looked up to breathe, it was midnight.

I stared at the painting in front of me.

A Paris Proposal.

No.

Dear Paris, I Propose.

Yes!

I like the sound of that better!

I smiled at my work.

It was clear that a proposal, my proposal, was happening in Paris, but the swirls of colors intensified the setting, making it something much more.

"Al! Al!" I screamed, already knowing he wouldn't hear me.

I stood up too fast, almost making myself dizzy, but still I ran up the basement stairs.

"Al!"

I headed towards the set of stairs that led upstairs to our bedroom, but I came to an abrupt halt once I caught sight of Al's foot hanging off the couch.

I should've known he wouldn't be too far away.

"Al?"

He opened one eye.

"Al, I painted something!"

"I know," he mumbled. "Did you throw it away?"

"Not that one. I painted something else!"

Al smiled. "Good." He pulled the blanket over his head.

"Get up! Get up and come and see it!"

"Now?" He mumbled underneath the covers.

"Now!"

Al groaned, but he got up from the couch.

My excitement caused him to slightly giggle as I led him towards the basement.

"Look! I'm calling it; *Dear Paris, I Propose.*"

I beamed at the beauty of the painting.

It isn't my best work.

And it's not something that I think Lula will like.

But it's most definitely beautiful!

And most importantly, it means that I haven't lost my gift!

"Wow! This is beautiful, Nema. It really is!" Al smiled. "We should put this in our bedroom."

"I thought I was broken, but I'm not! I thought I'd lost my talent, my gift, but I haven't! This---this proves that I still got it! I'm back! I'm back!" I jumped up and down like a kid in a toy store.

"I told you everything was going to be okay," Al yawned. "And now that you know that, hopefully you can paint your little heart away for a while, and then we can start working on our family."

Welp!

He completely ruined my moment!

"We talked about this, Al."

"I know. I was just hoping you changed your mind. You know, since you're not broken, as you said."

"I haven't. I don't want kids right now."

Al exhaled. "Okay, Nema."

I could hear the disappointment in his voice.

"Al, you're ruining the moment for me."

"What? How?"

"Nothing. Just nothing."

"No," Al groaned. "How? Because I said something about starting a family?"

"Yes! This wasn't the right time!"

"Then when is the right time?"

"I don't know! But this was *my* moment!"

Al shook his head. "When did you become so damn selfish?"

"Excuse me?"

Al headed up the stairs. I followed him.

"Selfish? I am not selfish!"

"Okay, Nema."

"No, it's not okay!"

"Yes!" Al yelled. "Yes, it is okay!"

"I'm not selfish! Not even a little bit! I have spent the past two years trying to be the perfect wife to you, so much so, that I neglected the things that I love! I made you my entire world!"

"I never asked you to do that!"

"You never told me not to either!" I screamed at him. "Not once did you tell me to stop cooking! Not once did you ask me to stop having sex with you whenever you wanted it! Not once did you ask me to stop giving you damn near all of my free time!"

"Wow. It's nice to know how much you hate being my wife."

"What? That's not what I'm saying!" I screamed.

"Just okay, Nema."

Al shook his head in what appeared to be disgust.

I exhaled. "Al, you know what? I can't give you what you want anymore."

"What?" Al questioned.

"What if I don't want kids for another five or six years? Or what if I never want them?"

Al didn't respond.

"I can't give you the version of me that you're used to right now, Al. Or maybe…maybe I can't give you that version of me ever again. I can't give you the woman that you married."

I walked towards the front door after grabbing my purse and keys off the coffee table.

"Nema?" Al called after me. "What are you doing? I swear if you do this…" Al took a deep breath. "What are you saying, Nema? What are you doing, huh?"

I opened the front door and without looking back at my husband, I answered him.

"I love you. I do. And I appreciate everything you have ever done for me. But I have to be honest. If you stay with me, for the next few years, you will probably be miserable until I feel like being the type of wife that I know you want me to be. The type of wife you deserve me to be. And right now, I just don't want to be her. And there's a possibility that I may never want to be her again. And I can't do that to you. I just can't. You don't deserve it. And I can't do that to you. Al...I want a divorce." I closed the door behind me without giving him a chance to say a word.

~***~

"You can stay here as long as you need to, but at least wash your ass!" Sophie pinched her nose. "It stinks in here! It's smells like fish, chips, and a whole bunch of other shit!"

For two days, I've been in Sophie's guest bedroom crying and refusing to get out of bed.

Al only called me once.

Once!

He called to make sure I was somewhere safe the night that I left. But since then, he hasn't said a word.

No calls.

No text messages.

Nothing.

This is not the response I was expecting from him.

I expected him to be doing any and everything to get me to come back home.

Maybe he's tired of my shit.

Tired of whatever this is that I'm going through.

Maybe, now, he wants a divorce too.

"You should call him."

"No. He doesn't want to talk to me."

"You don't know that."

I didn't respond.

"Are you going to work tomorrow?"

"Yes. I need you to go by the house and get some of my things."

"Tonight?"

"Yes. I need clothes. And can you grab some of my art supplies from the basement?"

"Girl, what if your husband tries to kill me or something? Rage and a broken heart make people do crazy things! I watch too much T.V. for this mess!" Sophie rolled her eyes. "What if I go over there trying to get your shit and he snaps?"

"Sophie..."

"What? It's a possibility."

"Al isn't like that."

Sophie shrugged. "Okay. Okay. I'll go. I'll just take Minnesota with me. Just in case."

Minnesota is Sophie's 9mm pistol.

"At least go sit in the bathtub until I get back. This room smells like stale pussy."

"Fuck you, Sophie."

"No. Fuck the stain in those panties you got on. I know there's one in them. There has to be."

Sophie laughed just before the pillow I threw at her hit her in the face.

I laid for a while longer, after Sophie was gone, and then to avoid hearing her mouth, I forced myself out of bed, and headed to take a bath.

Sophie's house is gorgeous!

It's bold, lavish and almost royal.

But the best rooms in the entire house are her bathrooms.

The guest bathroom is drizzled in gold and ivory. Between the gold-stained toilet, the huge gold and crystal chandelier, the gold bear claws on the bottom her gold and ivory marble bathtub, and the gold shimmer in the tiles on the floor…

Sophie's guest bathroom is fit for a queen.

And her bathroom is even more extravagant!

My body instantly relaxed once I sat in the bathtub full of scalding water.

Never did I ever imagine that I would be thinking about divorcing Al.

I got lucky.

I really did.

When Al asked for my phone number, instead of Sophie's, I knew he was different.

We stayed on the phone all night long, talking, laughing, and getting to know each other.

He must've called me beautiful a hundred times.

He called me beautiful so much that I didn't have a choice but to believe him.

But by the end of the night, I knew.

I knew that one day, he was going to ask me to marry him. I didn't know when, but I knew Al was going to be my husband.

I reached for my cell phone that was resting on the small table beside the bathtub. I called Sophie to make sure she was able to get some of my things. She told me Al already had a few of my bags packed and waiting for me by the front door. She said he'd even packed quite a bit of my art supplies, as well as my paper and easel.

According to Sophie, Al appeared to be just fine.

She said he and his friends were eating hot wings and watching wrestling on T.V.

I guess I assumed he would be sitting around as sad as I am but hearing that he was acting as though he didn't have a care in the world made me angry!

He's supposed to be worried about me!

He's supposed to be worried the outcome of our marriage! He's supposed to be sitting around, crying and thinking about us all day and night! Just like I've been doing for the past two days.

"Hello?" I'd said as soon as Al answered the phone.

"Yeah."

"Uh, what are you doing?"

"Nothing, Nema," Al said, dryly.

"You haven't called."

"I know."

I was trying my best not to go off on him.

I kept reminding myself that I'm the one who left him.

"So, that's it? This is it? You have nothing to say?"

Al didn't respond.

"Hello?"

"Yeah?"

"Did you hear what I said?"

"Yeah."

Al spoke to his friends.

I could tell that he was stepping away so that he could say whatever he wanted to say to me in private.

"So, we're getting a divorce?"

"Nema, I don't know what you want me to say. I didn't do anything wrong. And I don't want to argue with you. All I've ever tried to do is love you, and all of a sudden you don't want me anymore. I thought about begging you, chasing after you, crying, and everything else in between. Then, I realized something. Who wants to beg someone to be with them when they keep making it clear that they don't want to be? You don't want to be with me. And I can't make you, Nema. I can't make you want me. So, do whatever it is that you want to do, Nema, okay?"

"That's it? You're not going to fight for me? For us? You said that you would fight to the death of you to save us! That's what you said!"

"I want to fight. I tried to fight. But I can't fight by myself, Nema. I've done nothing wrong," Al explained.

"I never said you did anything wrong, Al. I told you, it's me. It's all me. I just thought you would at least try to help me figure things out."

"I tried. I tried to make you happy. I tried to help you get back to doing what you love. And you did it. You painted something beautiful. I tried, Nema. But that wasn't enough. You still weren't happy. You still didn't want us. And you still walked out on me," Al paused. "I gotta' go, Nema."

And with that, he hung up without saying goodbye.

He hates me!

My husband hates me!

And it's all my fault!

I cried loud and ugly until I heard the beeping sound signaling that Sophie was back and had opened the front door.

She yelled that she'd put all of my things in the guest bedroom from the other side of the bathroom door, and then for the next hour and a half, I just sat there, refilling the bathtub with hot water, over and over again, lost in a whirlwind of thoughts and silent tears.

Finally, I forced myself out of the bathtub.

I went through the bags that Al packed for me and realized how well my husband knows me.

I noticed how much he pays attention to me.

Al literally packed everything that I would've packed for myself from the clothes and shoes, to the underwear, and all the way down to the accessories and fragrances.

I couldn't believe that Al knew exactly what lotion and body sprays I would be looking to wear to work for the week, and he packed everything I would need.

Wow.

I checked the bag of art supplies.

Al packed all the necessities.

He watches me.

He studies me.

He knows me.

He…

Al truly loves me.

Once I was comfortable in my pajamas, I grabbed my art supplies, and headed out of the room.

I froze at the sight of Sophie, asleep on her indigo-colored sofa. She must've taken a shower while I was in the bathtub because she was now wearing a crimson-colored silk nightgown that hugged her body to perfection.

Her face was calm, but her beautiful jet-black curls were wild and untamed. She appeared comfortable, yet her pose was photoshoot ready. She was like a beauty and a beast, all combined into one.

Yes.

That's the best way to explain her, both physically and personality wise.

Sophie is and has always been one of the most beautiful pieces of art I've ever seen.

I smiled.

And then, I got an idea.

A few minutes later, I sat directly across from my sister, inspired with a sketching pencil in my hand.

I started to draw Sophie, exactly as she was in front of me. Once I drew her, I used my paintbrush and paint to embellish her beauty.

I was filled with so much anger, sadness and passion, all at the same time, but I couldn't stop painting.

My mind was all over the place, yet my eyes were deadlocked on Sophie, and my hands seemed to have a mind of their own. They moved swiftly, paint to paint, stroke to stroke. And as I put the finishing touches on the painting, I knew that I'd just created a masterpiece.

My heart was full as I named the painting out loud.

"The Sophie."

I smiled.

****

FOUR

I spy…

My husband with another woman.

I swallowed the lump in my throat.

I've been staying at Sophie's for almost a month now. Al and I have probably spoken a total of five times since I've been gone.

Honestly, though I made the decision to leave, I thought Al would be killing himself to get me back.

In the back of my mind, and though I'd said the words, I'd been prepared for Al to do just about anything to keep me from divorcing him.

But Al hasn't done a thing.

Literally, he's done absolutely nothing!

At all.

Even when we speak, he doesn't try to change my mind, nor does he ask me to come back home. Usually, he just listens to me talk, barely saying anything at all.

And now…

He's standing right there with another woman.

I called Al's cell phone to see if he would answer it.

Unaware that I was watching him from a distance, my husband looked down at his cell phone, and without answering it, he placed it in his back pocket.

I called him again as he laughed about something with the pretty, brown-skinned woman in front of him.

Who is she?

I stared at them through the window of the coffee shop as I called him over and over again.

Al never answered his phone.

Ugh!

I'm still his wife!

I marched towards the coffee shop's door, but suddenly, I stopped.

Al isn't that type of guy.

Al wouldn't start seeing someone else so soon.

He would wait until our divorce is final.

I think.

I hope.

So, whoever the woman is, I'm sure it's nothing romantic going on between them.

Then why isn't he answering my calls?

No.

There's no reason to think irrationally.

I know Al.

I know my husband.

Husband...

Does he even feel like my husband anymore?

I mean, I did ask him for a divorce.

If he is on a date or interested in this woman, what right do I have to go in there and confront him?

What would I say?

Instead of going inside the coffee shop, I turned away.

"Hey, you! Is everything okay?" Vanessa asked me later on at work that day.

"No. But it will be."

Vanessa eyed me suspiciously. "Spill it."

"What? I don't have anything to say," I mumbled.

Vanessa didn't believe me. "What happened? Who did it? Do you need me to whoop their ass?"

I chuckled.

"Seriously. Tell me. What's wrong? Did your husband forget your anniversary or something?"

Speaking of anniversaries, my wedding anniversary is only a little over a week away.

And from the looks of it, it'll be our second---and our last.

"Trust me, Al would never forget something like that. But as I said, I'm fine," I lied. "I'm just a little tired. That's all. Oh, are you busy tomorrow? I have a brunch to go to and I was wondering if you wanted to come with me."

Tomorrow is the day!

I'll be attending the brunch at Lula's house.

Unfortunately, the only painting I have that's good enough to take with me is the one of Sophie.

Surprisingly, I've managed to paint a few more while staying at Sophie's house these past few weeks, but none of the others even comes close to the one of my sister.

"I have a lunch date tomorrow."

"Oh really?"

"Yes, really. And girl, he's so sexy!" Vanessa squealed. "I'm nervous and excited, all at the same time! And I was going to ask you if you and Al could double date with us."

Keeping Vanessa in the dark about my separation with Al, is somewhat shady of me.

She truly is a great friend.

Over the past two years, we have laughed together.

Cried together.

We've even shared a few deep dark secrets with one another. She's a good listener. And I appreciate her friendship.

It just never seems like the right time to tell her about my situation. And now, after learning that she's finally dating again, I wouldn't want to discourage her.

Let's just say, Vanessa hasn't been so lucky with love.

"We can't go. Sorry. I have the brunch thing and I'm not sure if Al has anything planned for tomorrow or not."

I glanced down at my cell phone only to find that Al hasn't even bothered calling me back from earlier.

If I'm being honest, I miss his random text messages. No matter how busy he got during the day, Al always made time to text me something sweet, nasty, or a compliment.

I used to ask him to stop texting me so much while I was at work. He never listened, but I would get annoyed with him fifty percent of the time, especially if I was busy. Now, I see that he just wanted me to know that he was always thinking about me.

I'm such a bitch!

Sending him a random text message crossed my mind, but I'm unsure of what to say. And I don't want to seem like a pest. I can only imagine how confusing my actions are to him.

Hell, I'm confusing myself!

One day, I'm leaving him.

The next, I'm fussing at him for not trying to get me to stay. I'm just all over the place these days.

After a few more minutes of random conversation, Vanessa disappeared, and I found myself wanting to burst into tears. I slipped into the bathroom hoping to cry for a while, without anyone noticing I was gone.

About three minutes in, I heard someone enter the bathroom. Hurriedly, I stopped sniffling and wiped my face. A few minutes later, the toilet flushed in the stall next to me. I waited until they finished washing their hands, and once I heard the bathroom door closed, I came out of the stall.

I jumped at the sight of Diana standing next to the bathroom door with her arms folded across her chest.

"What's wrong with you?"

"Nothing."

I walked towards the sink.

"Liar." Diana said. "Why are you crying?"

"I'm not."

"Yea. And I'm not five-five, brown-eyed and bowlegged," she rolled her eyes.

"I'm surprised you even care," I snarled at her.

"What's wrong?"

"Nothing. I'm fine, Diana. And I would appreciate it if you didn't…"

"If I didn't what? Tell anyone I saw you crying?"

"Yes." I dried my hands. "Excuse me, Diana."

I grabbed the handle on the bathroom door, but Diana pushed it closed.

"Move."

She stared at me. "What is it about you that everyone loves?"

"Maybe if you get rid of your nasty attitude, people might actually like you too."

I pulled at the door handle again.

This time, Diana didn't try to stop me.

I walked out of the bathroom with a fake smile on my face and went back to work.

The remainder of the workday was long and depressing.

I couldn't get Al off my mind.

As soon as I walked out of the building, I called Al again. I called him three times, and once he finally answered, all hell broke loose!

Al and I argued for the next five hours!

I never mentioned seeing him with the woman at the coffee shop, but I did ask him if he was seeing someone else, and that just sent him into an everlasting rant.

He went on and on about how I left him, and how I didn't want him. He reminded me of our vows and yet again, he called me selfish. There was so much pain in his voice. And maybe even a little bit of hate too.

I tried to defend myself.

I tried to explain my actions and decisions. I tried to make him see my side of things and understand where I was coming from. I screamed at Al so much and for so long, that I started to lose my voice.

As expected, nothing was resolved and finally, Al said something that I thought he would never say.

"You win, Nema. Okay. You win. You've convinced me. And you were right. We should get a divorce. Are you happy now?"

That was the last thing he said to me before hanging up in my face.

I win?

Then why does it feel like I just lost the best thing that has ever happened to me?

I called Al back, but he didn't answer.

After calling him ten times in a row, finally, I gave up.

I text Al, three times, and then I turned off my cell phone to keep myself from texting him again.

Later that night, I laid wide awake, imagining my life without Al. I wondered if I would ever be the successful artist that I longed to be. I wondered if I would ever remarry, or if I would indeed ever have kids. I wondered if I would ever find love again or a man that's at least half the man Al is.

I won't.

I'm sure of it.

And my miserable future will be all my fault.

I'm the one who changed.

I'm the one who walked out on my marriage.

I'm the one who gave up on my husband.

And now, he's giving up on me too.

I guess divorce is the only one thing left to do.

~***~

"Why can't I see that one? I've seen all the other ones," Sophie complained.

"Because, if the buyer doesn't want this one, I'm going to give this one to you as a gift. That's when you'll see it."

The painting of Sophie has been hidden away in the guest bedroom closet for weeks. I hope Lula loves it, but if she doesn't, I know Sophie will.

After all, it is a painting of her.

"Whatever you say," Sophie shrugged. "Did you call about that building that I told you about? It would make the perfect art gallery or something for you to start selling your work."

"I'm nowhere near ready for an art gallery, Sophie. I don't have enough pieces. And they would have to be amazing, damn near brilliant pieces for me to even think about showcasing them for sale. But I did call, just out of curiosity. And to buy the building it's $250,000."

"You can always lease it, first. I leased first, remember? And when my boutique sales started to boom, I was able to buy the building."

"Maybe one day. We will see. As I said, I'm nowhere near ready for my own art gallery. I really have to get my mojo back before I start thinking that big."

"You've got it back, Nema. You've been painting or drawing something every single day. You are ready, even if you don't think you are," Sophie encouraged me. "It's your time to shine! It's your time to level up and become the boss bitch that I know you can be!" Sophie chuckled. "Now, go and sell that damn painting, girl!"

"I wish you could come with me," I whined.

"No, thanks," Sophie flopped down on the sofa. "I need my beauty rest. I have a long night ahead."

Sophie is hardly ever home.

She may stay home two or three days out of the week. The other nights, I'm there alone.

Some days, I don't see her at all unless I go by the boutique or if she comes by the auction house on my lunch break.

A few minutes later, I was out the door and following the GPS to Lula's house.

"Hello?"

I answered my cell phone.

It was a number I didn't recognize.

"Hello, naughty girl," he whispered.

"Hello?"

His breathing was intense.

"You're a bad, bad girl. And I like it!"

"Excuse me?"

The man laughed. "Whoops! I thought I called my wife!"

And with that, he hung up.

Surprisingly, I laughed.

It reminded me of the time I attempted to have phone sex with Al. It was a complete disaster!

It was at the very beginning of our relationship.

Listening to Sophie's freaky ass, I wanted to try something new. So, one night, I stayed over at Al's house. While he was watching a basketball game on T.V., I locked myself in his bedroom.

I called him, with my legs wide open, attempting to have phone sex with him while in the same house, but in different rooms. Needless to say, Al only lasted about two minutes before banging on the bedroom door.

When I refused to open it, he kicked it open, unaware that I'd gotten off the bed and was standing right behind the door. The door hit me in the face so hard that it broke my nose.

What was supposed to be something fun and sexy, ended up costing us a five-hour emergency room visit.

We never tried to have phone sex again.

Al apologized for weeks.

He bought me everything but a Rolls Royce to show me how sorry he was.

He's always had this type of over-the-top love, which is why it throws me for a loop that he isn't pulling out his bag full of tricks to fix us.

After driving down a long road for about two minutes, finally, I pulled up at Lula's house.

Well, more like mansion.

The gates opened and so did my mouth.

Lula's home is enormous!

And it's peach!

A big, peach, gated mansion out in the middle of nowhere.

It's so…so…Lula!

Lula asked me to arrive early so that she could see the painting, but there were already quite a bit of cars lined up behind each other in the long driveway.

"Hi. Am I late?" I smiled at Lula. She'd opened the front door before I could ring the doorbell.

"Oh, no! Most of those cars are mine. The others are my staff's for the evening. Come on in," she smiled noticing the wrapped canvas in my hand. "I can't wait to see it!"

I could barely focus on walking between trying to carry the painting and observing my surroundings.

Everything was so elegant.

So expensive!

A blind man could see that Lula has impeccable taste, which made me start to second guess showing her the painting in my hand.

"Okay, here. Here is where I need something outstanding!" Lula pointed to the empty space on the wall.

I glanced around the room.

It gave me a sort of royalty vibe.

Golds and reds.

Hmmm…

The painting just might do.

I took a deep breathe.

"You can open it," I gave the painting to Lula.

She didn't hesitate to rip off the brown paper covering the painting. Lula took a deep breath as soon as the painting was exposed and so did I.

"I call it: *The Sophie*."

"Your sister?"

"She was my inspiration."

I'd exaggerated a few features of Sophie's face in the painting, but it's still just as beautiful as she is.

Lula smiled and placed her hands over her mouth.

"Nema…I love it! I absolutely love it!"

"Really?"

"Hell, yeah! Really!" Lula continued to admire the painting and then she started to yell. "Savannah! Bring my checkbook! Phillipe! I have a new painting! You know what to do!"

Lula's workers came running.

The woman greeted me as she reached Lula her checkbook and a pen.

"How much?" Lula opened her checkbook.

"Uh…"

"Come on, don't be shy. That painting is beautiful! It's even better than *Paint Me Blue*. And one day, I'll most likely resell it for triple whatever I pay you," Lula laughed. "So, how much?"

"Lula, I honestly wasn't sure if you would like it so…"

Lula started to write.

"What about this? If you want more, just say the word."

I looked at the amount on the check and gasped. "$20,000?"

Lula smirked. "Yeah. You're right." She started to write on another check. She smiled as she reached it to me.

"$30,000? Oh, Lula, I can't. This is too much."

Lula smiled at Phillipe as he walked back in with the painting. It was now framed and protected by glass.

"Perfect! Hang it right there," Lula pointed towards the wall. "And you…" she turned to me. "If you don't believe in your work, no one else will. This piece is amazing! Cash both of those checks," she winked at me. "You earned them. You definitely deserve them! Pretty soon, I'll probably be writing you million-dollar checks for your work! Now, come on. Have a drink with me before the other guests arrive."

Still in shock that I was literally holding fifty-grand in my hand, I followed Lula towards the bar that was inside her house.

The man behind the bar fixed Lula and I a drink.

Lula smiled at him, in a sexual way. It was clear that she and the Jamaican bartender had something going on. And after staring at him for a few seconds too long, I started to see why. I would screw him too.

An hour or so later, women who looked like they'd stepped off the cover of a magazine started to pour into the room. I sat at a table, drinking mimosas, watching wealthy women chat, and well, be wealthy.

I felt terribly out of place.

I never really thought much about being rich before. I've thought about being famous, or well-known for my work, but I've never really pondered the idea of what it would truly be like to be extremely wealthy. Or what it would be like to have more money than I could probably spend in a lifetime.

But looking at these women, in diamonds and pearls, furs, and wearing newly released $5,000 pairs of shoes, I didn't have a choice but to wonder if I could ever be where they are someday.

Lula screamed in my direction.

She waved, frantically, for me to come to her.

Lula may be rich, now, but she's definitely still the same loud, carefree, tactless woman that I met in college.

No, I'm being nice.

Lula is ghetto as hell!

And she always has been.

I headed towards her.

I could feel the women judging me with their eyes.

"This is the woman behind this beautiful piece of art! It's custom-made! An original," Lula bragged.

"It's gorgeous!" the lady in the red dress, who I've been endlessly staring at, said to me.

"Thank you."

"Do you have any other pieces available? I would love to see them."

"Me too."

"Me three!"

"Uh, not---not currently," I stuttered. "I have a few that I'm working on."

Each of the ladies went inside of their purses or wallets to fetch me one of their business cards.

"I would love to see them when you're done. I love beautiful pieces of art."

Once my hands were full of their cards, they went back to talking to each other like I didn't exist.

It was as though I was suddenly invisible to them.

Slowly, I inched away, but just as I sat back down at the table, Lula joined me.

"Girl, you need to finish those pieces as soon as you can! They have plenty of money and they don't mind spending it! And I'm trying to get you some of it!" She laughed.

I smiled at her.

I've needed more people like Lula in my life these past few years, and I regretted losing touch with her for so long.

From what I remember about Lula, she came from an interesting, but loving family.

In college, her parents were still married.

She had one brother, and a family dog named Vodka.

She said her grandma started calling the dog Vodka, and it somewhat stuck.

Lula's parents were very different from mine.

My parents were structured.

They wanted us to be ready for the world.

Lula's parents were…

Just like Lula.

Loud.

Free-spirited.

Ghetto.

And they had the most cookouts I've ever seen!

Even in the winter, they would decide to have a house full of people and throw something on the grill.

Lula and her mom were more like friends than mother and daughter. Once, I heard her tell her mama to shut up and leave her alone.

My mama would've left me alone al'right.

She would've left me alone, with the mortician, at the funeral home, to prepare my body for my burial.

There's no way in hell I would've ever talked to my parents that way, but Lula could.

She also told me that she'd been allowed to have boys in her bedroom since she was sixteen years old.

We were raised completely different, yet Lula's outlook on life, in some ways, were admirable to me back then.

She lived day to day.

She lived worry-free.

She was never afraid to just go for it. And she was never, and I do mean never afraid to ask for what she wanted.

Lula was never ashamed of where she came from or ashamed of who she was. And from what I can tell, rich and all, she's still the same way.

The other women noticed that Lula had made her way over to me, so, they decided to join us at the table.

"How long have you been married?" One of the women asked me out of nowhere. Mostly likely because I'd been fondling with my wedding ring, which is something I do when I'm feeling nervous, excited or overwhelmed.

"Almost two years. But…" I hesitated.

I surely shouldn't be telling strangers my business.

But after examining the rings on most of their fingers, maybe I could get some martial advice. "We're headed towards a divorce."

"Shit, join the club," one of the women laughed. "We've all been divorced, at least once, and some of us are headed that way again." All of the women at the table nodded their heads. "Marriage isn't all its hyped up to be."

"Yeah. It's a lot harder than I thought it would be."

"What did he do?" Lula asked.

"Huh?"

"Your husband. What did he do to make you want a divorce?"

"Did he lie?" The lady in red asked.

"No."

"Cheat? Probably with his secretary."

"Nope."

"Is he gay? And you just found out?" Lula sipped her drink.

"No. Actually. He's perfect. It's me who wanted the divorce."

"By perfect what do you mean?" The woman who wore a big emerald ring on her finger spoke. "Please describe this perfect man to us."

"Well," I cleared my throat. "He's attractive. Hardworking. Sensitive. A great provider. He can cook and clean, just as good, if not better, than I can. He's loyal. Spontaneous. Adventurous. Generous. He's caring. Attentive…"

"Wait, wait, wait," Lula interrupted me. "And you don't want him?"

"Shit, I want him!" One of the ladies yelled and everyone else laughed.

"His sex must be horrible."

"Nope. He's in my top three, ever, in that department."

"He has a lot of kids and their mother's cause a lot of drama."

"Nope. No kids."

"Then excuse my French but…honey, what the fuck is wrong with you?"

The ladies laughed at me again.

Trying not to become offended, I tried to explain myself.

"Trying to love him, I lost myself. Trying to be perfect, like him, left me burnt out and empty. And I just can't give him what he wants and needs anymore."

"I'll give him whatever he wants. And baby, I'll take care of all of his needs! I can promise you that!" The woman wearing the emerald yelled.

"How much you want for him?" The lady in red mumbled.

"Huh?"

"You just described the perfect man. I'm on my way to my second divorce, and you don't want him…so how much do you want for him?"

"Let me get in on this too!" Another lady said.

I looked at Lula. She shrugged with a smile.

"Uh…"

"Every single, and unhappily married woman is looking for a man just like your husband."

All of the women at the table nodded their heads.

"If you're serious about divorcing him, how much would it cost for an introduction?"

"Are you ladies serious?"

"As serious as the millions in their bank accounts," Lula confirmed. "Shoot, we all want a good man, for once. I know I do. I'm tired of the rich assholes. Give me a normal, average, good-looking man, any day."

The lady wearing all white who hadn't spoken at all, stood up and with burning red lips she smiled. "If you get serious about this, I'll put my offer in too. Lula knows how to get in contact with me."

I enjoyed the rest of the brunch and Lula asked me to stick around once everyone else was gone.

"Do you feel inspired after some of the speeches?"

"Actually, I do. To see and hear the stories of so many successful black women is exhilarating! And not all of them became rich by marriage."

"Nope. Some of them are some real boss bitches," Lula laughed.

"I see that."

"And you…are you a boss?"

"I want to be. I really, really want to be," I believed the words coming out of my mouth. "My sister came across the perfect building that I could turn into an art gallery."

"I'll definitely be one of your best customers!" Lula eyed the painting of Sophie. "You truly have a gift. This painting really is a masterpiece. Go for it, Nema. If you want it, go for it! You can do it!"

"Thank you."

Lula turned her attention back to me. "I hope the girls didn't scare you."

"How? About the divorce thing? Oh, no. I know they were just kidding."

"Actually…they weren't. They were serious. Very, very serious."

I stared at Lula.

"Women with money will pay for what they want. No matter what that it," Lula started. "Love, real love, it's all so hard to come by these days. Marriage isn't what it used to be. And these so-called husbands are something else! They marry for their own selfish reasons, whether they're actually ready to be a husband or not. But you, you seem to have a good one that for whatever reason, you don't want. A good man that you're literally throwing away. So, why not turn your trash, into your treasure?" Lula suggested "They meant what they said. If you really don't want him, you could end up "selling" him to one of them, so to speak. Who knows, you might have that art gallery sooner than you think."

Not knowing how to respond, I didn't say anything.

I simply let Lula talk my head off as I made my way towards the door.

"Keep in touch, Nema! Especially if you paint something amazing…or if you get that divorce sooner than later!"

Once I was inside my car, I stared at the two checks Lula had given me.

The checks combined are only $10,000 less than my yearly salary at the auction house.

I placed the checks safely back inside my purse, and drove away slowly, constantly glancing at the peach mansion in my rearview mirror.

I couldn't exactly explain what I was feeling inside.

I just know that whatever it is, I like it.

The inspiration.

The want to have a seat at the table.

The burning fire inside my belly to became as successful and as wealthy as the women I met today.

The want to have even my wildest dreams come true.

All of it.

Sometimes, we never really know what we want until we actually see it.

Today, I saw it.

And I want it.

I want it all.

And I'm going to use my talent to get it!

~***~

"We'll all be divorced soon. Wow," Gia said.

She and Paul are now officially divorced.

"Ours should be final next week," Cathy chimed in. "I hear the ball should be rolling on yours pretty soon." She added looking at me.

"Oh, I haven't even filed yet."

"Al did. Or at least he's planning to," Cathy looked as though she had just put her foot in her mouth. "Wait, you did know this, right?"

Al already filed for a divorce?

Really?

Being in Georgia, once I left the house, and being that I stated I wanted a divorce, Al can definitely file.

But since I'm the one who asked for a divorce, I thought…

"I could be wrong. I walked in on the end of the conversation between the guys. All I heard Al say was that the papers were going to be filed, and that he was going to let you have the house. He could have been speaking future-wise. I just thought he meant he was the one filing for the divorce, although you're the one who wanted it."

Our two-year anniversary is tomorrow.

I started to hyperventilate.

The girls immediately tried to comfort me.

"Nema, do you really want this? Do you really want a divorce?"

I shrugged.

This past week, I've been drawing and painting like crazy.

If I'm feeling sad, I draw.

If I'm feeling mad, I paint.

If I start to miss Al or start to get overwhelmed thinking about what the next few years of my life may look like, I draw and paint some more.

And just to toot my own horn, every painting from the past week has been nothing shy of amazing!

"You can stop this. There's still time to fix it," Gia said. "Al is a different breed. He's worth keeping. He's worth fighting for."

"I know. Believe me, I know."

"Then keep him," Cathy suggested.

I really wish it was that simple.

Or maybe it is.

We finished our dinner, and on the long ride home to Sophie's house, I thought about saving my marriage.

I thought about what staying married to Al would look like in the next few years.

I pictured a baby girl.

I could see a huge grin on Al's face as he held her.

I could see this glow of happiness all over him.

I'll admit, it made me smile.

All he has ever wanted is me.

All he has ever wanted is our family.

Maybe he still does.

Maybe he's just waiting.

He's waiting for me to fight. Or maybe he's just waiting for a sign that I still want our marriage.

I arrived at Sophie's house to find a strange man standing on her front porch.

He approached me as soon as I got out of the car.

"Hey, do you know if Sophie is inside?" He asked nervously. "I wasn't sure if her car was just in the garage or if she's really not here."

"Did you ring the doorbell?"

"Yes. But she didn't come to the door. And she isn't answering her cell phone. Could you call her?"

"Who are you?" I questioned him.

"A friend."

"Does "a friend" have a name?"

"Maz."

I took out my cell phone and called Sophie.

"Hey, Soph, I just got to your house and there's a Maz here looking for you."

"I know. I'm sitting in the living room watching my show," Sophie said unbothered. "He's one of my regular stalkers. He pops up once a month or so. Although, I haven't talked to him or had sex with him in almost a year."

What the hell?

"Okay, I'll let him know."

I looked at the middle-aged man, with the salt and pepper beard standing in front of me.

He's beautiful.

If men can be such a thing.

But apparently, he's crazy too.

"Uh, Sophie is out and she says she probably won't come home tonight."

"Cool."

Without another word, he walked away, got into his black Mustang and drove away.

What in the hell does Sophie do to these men?

From the things she says, I've always known that my sister is a freak. And from what she's told me, nothing in the bedroom is off limits.

Sophie licks booty holes and all...with her nasty ass!

She says that while she's giving head, she eases down to the man's balls, and while she's down there, she slips her tongue in and out of his butthole.

According to her, she says that men love it, and that licking their asses makes their dick extra hard.

Fuck that!

I'll fuck a broomstick before I lick a man's asshole.

But Sophie does it, and I think she likes it.

Men can't get enough of her.

I guess being pretty and nasty is one hell of a combo.

I walked into the house to find Sophie in a bonnet with a big bowl of popcorn on her lap.

I stared at her.

"What?" She shrugged.

"Girl, you just have strange men popping up at your house?"

"Honey, he's the third one to pop up since you've been living here. You were just out when the other two came by."

"Really? That's crazy! What do they want?"

"Me," Sophie said nonchalantly. "I have a handful of stalkers that just won't go away. They're the reason why I don't bring men to my house anymore. Or tell them that I own a boutique. Now, I just pretend to be you. I tell them that I work a nine to five at an auction house."

"Oh, hell no! Don't be using me!" I frowned. "Wow, Soph. Why are they coming by here? Do they still want to be with you?"

"Duh," Sophie laughed. "Of course, they still want me."

"And why don't you want them? Were you dating them, or just screwing them?"

"A mixture of both. If they're not the one…I have fun. And then, I let them go. I'm looking for the one."

"You and this whole *the one* thing."

"Well, it's the truth. The perfect man for me is out there somewhere. And I'm going to find him. Or he's going to find me. Either way, that's who I'm waiting on. And if a man isn't it…well, he's just not it."

"If you say so," I exhaled. "Well, I'm going to take a shower, and get ready for bed. I have a long day at work tomorrow."

"Oh, you won't be getting any sleep tonight."

"What?"

"You'll see," Sophie said.

By the time I took a shower, and slipped into my pajamas, the doorbell started to ring over and over again.

"Sophie, someone is at the door!"

"I know," she answered. "It's Maz."

"I told him you weren't here."

"He doesn't care. And he doesn't believe you. He's going to ring that doorbell for hours," Sophie turned up the T.V.

The doorbell continued to ring.

"Sophie, you need to call the police!"

She chuckled. "He is the police." Sophie patted the couch beside her. "Come on. Have a seat. He'll leave in a few hours."

"In a few hours? Oh, hell no! I'm going out there to tell him to go away!"

"He won't. And he's the Police Chief. No one can make him. Have a seat, sister," Sophie coached me.

"You slept with the Police Chief?"

Sophie shrugged.

Extremely annoyed, I sat down beside her, and tried my best to tune out the sound of the doorbell.

Sophie focused on T.V. and I almost felt sorry for her. Whatever it is that she does to men, to make them act like this about her…I wouldn't wish this type of unwanted attention on my worst enemy.

From 9:56 p.m. until 1:14 a.m. Maz rang the doorbell nonstop. And then finally, it came to an abrupt end.

After ten minutes of silence, Sophie spoke.

"Hmm, he stopped early. He must've got called into work or something." She headed to look out the window. "Yeah. He's gone," she exhaled. "Thank goodness. At least he won't be back for another month or so. He only comes when his wife goes out of town to visit her folks once a month. And before you say something, he wasn't married when we started fooling around. Engaged, but not married. I didn't even know about the engaged part until he tried to call off his wedding to marry me. I already knew he wasn't the one though, so, I told him to marry her. I told him we were done. And yet, he just can't let go."

Exhausted, I yawned, and without responding to Sophie, I headed to get a few hours of sleep before it was time to get up for work.

Hours later, and after two cups of coffee, I was headed out the door towards the auction house.

It's my anniversary.

And I feel like shit!

I was supposed to be off for a whole week, because I wasn't sure what Al had planned, but I changed my vacation days to the end of the month instead.

I wonder if Al would call, or text, but so far, he hasn't said a word.

Two years married, today, and we're not even speaking to each other.

In a horrible mood, I arrived at work, only to find tons of trucks out front. There were about ten men in uniforms loading inventory from the auction house onto the trucks.

"Good, okay, she's here," Connie the owner of the auction house said once she noticed me.

The other employees and I, all five of us, waited on her to speak.

"Unfortunately, today is everyone's last day."

Everyone started to talk at once.

"I know, this is a surprise. Imagine my surprise when I found out my husband and my business partner are sleeping together," Connie confessed. "They've been having an affair for years. Right under my nose."

My heart dropped.

Immediately, I felt sorry for her.

"Any who, everything is out, and this move has to be made. I don't want to see either of them ever again. My marriage is over. My friendship with Giselle is over. And so is this partnership. So…we've sold all of our pieces to other auction houses, and we're closing down immediately." Connie said. She fondled with the envelopes in her hand. "I know this is sudden, and I know no notice was given. And because of that, I've decided to compensate all of you with sort of a severance pay, until you find something else." Connie tapped the piece of paper on a table behind her. "By taking these checks, you agree that you won't try to sue me, or anything of that nature. What's in these envelopes are half of your yearly salaries, which is probably more than any of you would get from unemployment."

Half of my yearly salary…

That's about thirty thousand dollars for me.

"You have to sign this notarized document first, and the checks are yours," Connie didn't look happy at all. "I'm sorry for this, I truly am. I appreciate each of you and all you've done around here. I can't believe that my dream is coming to an end. This is not what any of us expected. But this is it. This is the end. Maybe if I hadn't been too busy dreaming, I would've been awake long enough to see what was happening in my house and in my bed."

"Give me a pen," Vanessa was the first to speak up.

The rest of us followed.

I looked at the check inside the envelope.

Just like that, I'm unemployed.

But I am sitting on a pretty penny.

To date, I haven't cashed the checks for selling my painting to Lula. And now, I have another check to go with them. I placed the severance check inside my purse.

"I'm sorry," Connie teared up. "Take care everyone. I'm sorry."

And with that she ran out of the building.

A part of me wanted to run after her.

But what am I going to say?

My marriage is a mess too.

"Well, this isn't how I expected my day to go," Diana grumbled. "But I've been tired of coming here for a while now. Good riddance."

Vanessa and I stayed behind for a while, watching the men carry out each item, piece by piece.

"I can't believe we won't be working together anymore," Vanessa frowned. "Now, I'll hardly ever get to see you."

"Oh, no. We will see each other all the time. I promise," I smirked at the sight of the hickey on her neck. "Looks like somebody has been getting busy!"

Vanessa noticed what I was looking at.

She blushed.

"Girl, oh, my God! I like him so much! He's so amazing! He really is. I have to tell you about him!"

Vanessa spilled her guts as we started to walk towards the exit. Just for a moment, I paused to look behind me.

The auction house served its purpose in my life.

This chapter of my life is ending.

And a new chapter is about to begin.

Goodbye.

Outside, I turned my attention back to Vanessa.

"So, what's his name?"

"Benny. Oh, he's just the man I've been looking for! I get so excited, and horny, every time I think about him!" Vanessa bit her bottom lip.

"Eww! T.M.I." I grinned at her. "But it's good to see you so happy."

"It's all so new, so I don't want to jinx it or anything. But I've been waiting on the right man for so long, and I think I've found him! I pray that I've found him! I really do!"

Vanessa was married once before.

Before I met her.

From what she's shared with me about her ex-husband, he was a liar and a cheater. And he left her in a very dark place. She'd wanted her marriage to work so badly, that she took his emotional and mental abuse for almost ten years. And still, in the end, he's the one who left her.

He divorced Vanessa and married another woman the day after their divorce was final.

It took Vanessa years to pick up the pieces of her life and to overcome depression.

"It just feels so good to finally be happy. And I'm so happy! So, we will see. Fingers crossed, chica!" Vanessa hugged me. "Please don't go ghost on me. You're one of my best friends. And I need you in my life. Tell Al he's going to have to share you. And I mean it!"

I smiled at her.

Now is the perfect time to tell her the truth about my marriage, but she's in such a happy place right now. And I refuse to ruin it.

"Well, let me go and cash this check! Call me later?"

"Absolutely."

Just as I got inside my car, Sophie called.

"Hey, Soph, can I call you back?"

"Girl, you have lost your husband."

"What?"

"Look at your phone."

A picture message from Sophie popped up.

It was a picture of Al…

And the woman I saw him with at the coffee shop that day. And with them was a little boy. No more than five, maybe six.

Al and the woman were sitting on a bench at the park and Al appeared to be teaching the boy how to properly hold a football. He had the biggest, happiest grin on his face that I've ever seen.

She, whoever she is, was smiling too.

Only she wasn't smiling at the boy. She was looking and smiling at Al.

My Al.

My heart dropped.

Ouch!

"Look at this one," Sophie said.

She sent another picture.

In this picture, the woman and Al were sitting close.

Very close.

And they were laughing about something.

Al's smile was big, and his head was slightly tilted back. She appeared to be laughing so hard that it made her eyes close. The small boy was on the grass in front of them, playing with the ball.

Is he dating her?

I didn't think Al would try to move on with anyone so soon; especially since we're still married.

I thought this lady I saw him with was nobody.

Obviously, I was wrong.

And of all days, he's out, at the park with her today.

But it's our anniversary!

Tears slowly rolled down my face.

"I told you, Nema. Even good guys don't wait forever. And I'll be damned if he doesn't look happy. He does look happy. Right? It's not just me."

That's the problem.

He does.

Sophie and I got off the phone, and I just sat there, full of sadness and rage.

He could've at least divorced me first!

When I'd thrown out the accusation that he could be seeing someone else, during our separation, Al denied it.

He lied to me.

Obviously.

I mean, clearly, it's no coincidence seeing him with the same woman, twice.

And she has a son.

I'm assuming the boy is her son.

Is this why he's filing for the divorce instead of waiting around for me to do it?

He's ready to move on and have everything he's ever wanted. Meanwhile, I just lost my job and I have no idea what my next move is going to be.

My phone started to vibrate.

It was Lula.

My mind was racing.

Just knowing that Al is already seeing someone else really hurt my feelings. Even if he'd told me the truth when I asked him, my feelings would've still been hurt, but at least he would've been honest.

He's a liar!

And, again…

It's our goddamn anniversary!

My phone stopped vibrating for only a second before it started to buzz again.

"Lula?"

"I just saw a story about your auction house on the news," she said.

"Never mind that," I said.

Al wants to move on?

Fine!

But he's going to move on, on my terms, to my benefit, and with the woman of *my* choice!

And little Ms. Chocolate Mama at the Park is not it!

How about that?

"Gather your friends and tell them it's on!"

"What? What are you talking about, Nema?" Lula questioned.

"I'm saying…" I paused as I looked at the picture of Al, the woman, and the boy again. "I'm saying exactly what you think I'm saying. I have a husband for sale. So…let the bidding begin!"

~***~

Instead of using my key, I rang the doorbell.

Al opened the door.

He was fresh out the shower and wearing only a towel.

I inhaled the scent of his skin.

I miss his smell.

I miss his touch.

I miss him.

Stay focused, Nema.

"Happy anniversary," I muttered.

Al stared at me.

He appeared to be examining my face.

I'm sure he could tell that I'd been crying for the past four hours.

After setting up a lunch date with Lula to discuss selling my husband, I went to the park.

The same park Sophie saw Al and the woman, but by the time I got there, Al, the woman, and the boy, were nowhere in sight.

So, for the past four hours, I just sat there, in my car, crying my eyes out.

"I was going to call…but I didn't know what to say," Al said finally. "Especially…."

Al walked away from the door as I stepped inside.

I miss home.

Al came back holding an envelope.

"Wow," I swallowed the lump in my throat.

I knew exactly what was in his hands.

Divorce papers.

"Nema," Al breathed heavily. "We can tear these papers up, right here, right now. The choice is yours."

I noticed my painting, *Dear Paris…I Propose*, sitting on the kitchen table with trash on top of it.

"I never wanted this. You did. But whatever game you're playing, I'm not playing it. So, like I said, the choice is yours."

Al waited for me to take the envelope.

He filed for divorced, just like Cathy said.

I know I'm the one who walked out but…

"Is it because of someone else?"

"What?" Al asked, instantly annoyed. "No. This is what YOU wanted, Nema! YOU!" Al turned his back to me. "See, this is what I'm saying. You and your mind games. It's ridiculous, Nema. It really is. And I don't have time for it. I'm a good man. And I'm not going to deal with this."

Al took a seat on the couch, still only wearing a towel.

I just stood there as Al looked at me in pure disgust.

I messed up.

I really messed things up.

"I feel like I don't know you anymore," Al said, interrupting my thoughts. "But you have the papers. I didn't want anyone to serve you. I wanted to give them to you myself. I wanted to let you know that despite all of this craziness, the choice is still yours."

No, it isn't.

If the choice was mine, he wouldn't have filed for a divorce in the first place.

Not saying a word, I walked towards him.

"We should be in Cancun right now. That's what I was planning for our anniversary. A trip to Cancun. I'd been planning it for months before…"

Now, standing directly in front of him, I felt a shitload of sadness and regret. Rage was still there, somewhere in the mix, but more than anything in the world, at this very moment, I wanted my husband to want me.

Even if it's just for a moment.

Even if it's temporary.

Even if it's for the last time.

Slowly, right in front of him, I started to undress.

"Nema? What are you doing?" Al questioned me.

I didn't say a word.

"Stop. Put your clothes back on." Al rubbed his dick, signaling that he was getting turned on. "Nema?"

Slowly, I pulled my shirt over my head and just as I was about to unfasten my bra, Al grabbed me by the shoulders.

"Stop! Nema, Stop!" He yelled. "I don't want you, not like this. I want all of you. Not just this! Just stop!"

Al released me, and to my surprise, without saying another word, he stormed away, heading up the stairs.

Seconds later, I heard what I assumed to be our bedroom door slamming shut.

Tears streamed down my face.

My marriage is over.

I got dressed in sadness, but anger met me at the kitchen table once I picked up my painting.

Stains were all over it.

Seeing that Al hadn't taken care of it, only made me feel like my feelings for wanting to leave him in the first place were valid.

My true happiness doesn't matter to him.

With my painting in one hand, and the divorce papers in the other, I walked out of the house feeling completely in control of my destiny.

And in control of his.

****

FIVE

"We will hold the "husband auction" a week from today," Lula smiled.

The divorce is happening.

The papers are signed.

Al and I haven't spoken since the meeting with our lawyer, weeks ago. And we didn't really speak then.

Our lawyer did most of the talking, and we both just sat there, staring at each other.

I feel like I've made the biggest mistake of my life.

I'm not sure if Al feels the same thing.

Our entire meeting, his phone chimed.

Text messages.

It was her.

I know it was her.

"Are you sure about this?" Lula asked.

"I have to be."

The auction is simple.

I'm selling Al to the highest bidder.

And then, I will tell the buyer everything there is to know about Al. I'll give her the inside scoop on him. Tell her his likes and dislikes. And show her things that she can do to get his attention, and hopefully, capture his heart.

Simply put...

I'll teach her how to be me.

It's understood that I can't make Al notice her or date her. But I can send her to places that I know he's going to be, help her get his attention, and make her overall the perfect woman for my soon-to-be ex-husband.

It's simple.

It's crazy.

It's out of the normal.

And honestly, it's a tad bit immoral, but Al started this war, and I'm going to finish it!

As long as the woman from the coffee shop and park doesn't have him, I'll be fine!

I saw how he looked at her in the coffee shop that day.

He used to look at me just like that.

So, nope!

She can't have him!

I'd rather one of these desperate rich bitches have him instead!

Since there are no guarantees, there's a good chance that I'll be getting paid for nothing.

As stated, I can't make Al want to be with them. I have no control over the outcome of all this. But if someone wants to throw away money by giving it to me, all because they hope a good man will take notice in them...

I'm sure as hell going to let them!

"Everything will be final next week. The day after the auction."

Since signing the divorce papers, I've painted fourteen extraordinary paintings. About twenty more, and a big fat check from one of these rich bitches, and I just might be able to open an art gallery after all.

Sooner than later.

Pain deserves all the credit for my latest masterpieces.

Pain is what was missing.

Being married to Al was painless.

We rarely argued. And when we did, he went out of his way to make things better.

Now, I see that a little pain, frustration, rage, and anger is what I needed in order to get back to creating. And now that I'm there, again, my artwork is better than it's ever been.

"Oh, and I have some new paintings if you want…"

"Yes! Bring them with you! As many as you can!" Lula clapped her hands in excitement. "You'll be selling your husband, and some new paintings! Yes! I love it! I can't wait!"

We finished our third lunch this month, and I headed to Sophie's boutique.

"Ooh, La, La!" Sophie squealed when she saw me. "You are looking super cute! You most definitely don't look like a woman who is about to be divorced!"

Living with Sophie, I've definitely tried to keep up, appearance wise. It's hard not to want to look pretty when you watch someone else get dolled up, every single day. Besides, I got tired of Sophie calling me Grandma Nema.

I was wearing a sleeveless orange and white jumpsuit, gold accessories, and gold open-toe wedges.

Sophie finished helping a customer, and then she gave me a hug.

"Girl, this is what I like to see! Show off those curves! You're about to be single and if you're going to snag yourself a new man, you gotta' show them what you're working with!"

"A new man is the furthest thing from my mind right now."

"For now. Once that sex-less pussy gets to thumping, you'll be on the prowl." Sophie laughed. "Oh, I want you to watch this new movie with me tonight."

I like living at Sophie's house.

Al tried his best to get me to take the house, but I refused. I don't want it.

Besides, living with Sophie keeps my mind off negative things. It's almost impossible to sulk around her. Sophie isn't the emotional type, at all. And she expects everyone else to be as tough as she is.

If I want to cry, I have to lock myself in the bathroom, or cry silently in bed. And if I even think I'm going to sit around all day and feel sorry for myself, Sophie will drag me out of the house, kicking and screaming, if she has to.

"Okay. I was---"

Sophie placed up one finger in my face as she answered her cell phone. She smiled, big, as soon as she placed the phone on her ear.

"Hey, you," she said.

Her face was full of excitement, happiness, and maybe even love.

My relationship is coming to an end.

And from the looks of it, Sophie's is just beginning.

I told Sophie I would see her later at home.

Not working during the day is boring.

But I'm somewhat thankful that I don't have to go to work while dealing with my divorce.

I could only imagine how draining it would've been to have to wear a fake smile all day long, when in actuality, especially in the beginning, I felt like dying inside.

Just as I got into my car, I spotted Al's and my friends across the street.

Gia and Jack.

What?

Gia and Paul are divorced now.

Jack and Cathy are divorced too.

And now…

Gia and Jack kissed each other.

Oh, my God!

Is this why they really divorced their spouses?

Were they having an affair the whole time?

How could they do this to Cathy and Paul?

Gia and Jack continued to kiss each other on the sidewalk, as though they didn't have a care in the world.

"Where is my phone? Where is my phone?" Frantically, I searched for my cell phone inside my purse. "I have to call Al."

With my phone now in my hand, just before pressing Al's name, I paused.

Should I call him?

This isn't my business.

And Al…isn't my husband.

At least he won't be soon.

Instead of calling Al, I placed my cell phone back inside my purse and drove right past my friends as though they didn't exist.

~***~

"That's stunning," I heard behind me.

I'd decided to go my favorite park and paint for the day.

It's late November.

And chilly.

So, I knew the park would practically be empty.

"Thank you," I looked behind me.

His height was overwhelming, but his smile was full of so much warmth that it caused my body to overheat.

The man standing behind me was light-skinned, with a neatly trimmed beard, and a massive chest.

Yum!

"No problem. It's full of so much passion. And maybe a little pain."

"Exactly," I smiled at the painting. "Are you an artist?"

"No, but I know a fine piece of art when I see one. I have quite the collection of paintings myself," he bragged just as he pulled out his cellphone. He squatted down and started to swipe through photos of his collection of paintings.

"Oh, my God! This one is absolutely amazing! Who's the artist?"

That was the start of a two-hour long conversation.

He, Germany is his name, sat on the grass beside me as I finished my painting.

He talked to me, gave me a few suggestions, and overall, made my entire afternoon.

"This painting is going to make you a lot of money. Watch and see," he said.

"I couldn't have gotten it this perfect without you. Can I name it after you?"

He smiled the brightest smile. "Sure. Under one condition."

"What is that?"

"You give me your phone number."

Am I blushing?

"Um, I'm in the middle of a divorce. It won't be final for another three days. And…"

"Then I'll call you on the fourth day."

"How did things go at the park? Did you paint something new?" Sophie asked once I sat down at the restaurant.

My siblings and I were having dinner together for the fifth time this month. Honestly, I think we're all just going through some things and who better to lean on than your brother and sister?

Even Cam seems full of frustration these days. I 'm not sure if it's marital related but getting together tonight was his idea.

"Actually, I did. It's probably one of my best. I'm calling it *Germany's Smile*."

"Oooh, I like that," Sophie smiled.

"So, how are you feeling? The divorce is final this week, right?" Cam changed the subject.

"Yes. And I don't know what to feel," I answered honestly. "Yesterday, Al left everything that I'd left at our house on Sophie's front porch."

Sophie nodded.

"He hates me. And that's hard for me to accept. I texted him last night, and he didn't respond. Guess it's out with the old and in with the new for your buddy Al," I grunted. "But I did this. So, I have to deal with it."

"Yeah. But girl, how do you get over the fact that he already has a pretty, brown-skinned thing on his arm? Chile, that would have me feeling some kind of way. I always thought you would be the one to move on first. I guess Al said fuck that. Life is too short," Sophie took a bite of her dinner roll.

"Oh, Al is dating already?" Cam asked.

"It looks that way."

"Damn. He didn't mention that to me. But I can see why. I am your brother."

"You've talked to him?" My heart skipped a beat.

"Yeah. I just wanted to check on him and see how he was doing."

"What did he say?"

I made Cam tell me, word for word, the conversation between him and Al.

"He is angry with you, though. But I understand. He loved you, Nema."

"Loved," I repeated.

"Loves," Cam corrected himself. "He still loves you, whether you believe that or not. He doesn't really want this. And neither do you."

I shrugged. "Nothing I can do about it now."

"Yes, there is. It ain't over, until it's over. If you don't want a divorce, just say so."

I didn't respond.

Sophie cleared her throat and changed the subject.

"So, are we opening up this art gallery or not? You know you can just borrow whatever you don't have from me," she said. "I know how you are about borrowing money. That's why I didn't suggest it before. But now, with you being divorced and all, you gotta' make things happen. By any means necessary."

I went from not being able to paint anything, painting at least three or four paintings a week.

"I'm really thinking about it. And I won't need to borrow. I'll have the money, if I choose to go that route."

"Oh, so, you do have two hundred-grand in the bank? Or are you just going to lease the building?"

"We will see, Sophie."

If I go through with this whole auctioning off Al thing, I shouldn't need to borrow anything from anybody, anytime soon.

According to Lula, I shouldn't be scared to start the bid for Al less than twenty-grand. She says she expects me to walk out of her house with a six-figure check, at the least.

Lula says that some of the women are so unhappy, whether single or still married, that they are eager for the opportunity to meet a man like Al.

Mentally, I checked out for the rest of dinner.

I laughed and smiled, and said a few words here and there, but mentally, my mind was everywhere else.

Especially on Al.

We could change our minds.

Right?

We could decide that we don't want the divorce and just stop it all.

I'm not sure if it works that way, but maybe it does.

Maybe we could…

After dinner, I told Sophie that I would be home later, and I headed towards the place that I used to call home.

I was going to see Al.

One last conversation.

One last shot.

I arrived at the house to find a car that I didn't recognize in the driveway. Without hesitating, I got out of my car and started to head towards the front door.

Before I could make it up the porch steps, the front door opened, and out came Al...

And her.

I froze, watching them as they laughed, waiting for them to notice me.

Once they did, her smile remained on her face.

Al's was instantly erased.

I just stood there.

"Hi," the woman said.

I didn't respond.

"Uh, Michelle, this is my ex-wife Nema. Nema, this is Michelle."

Ex-wife.

He called me his ex-wife a few days early.

Al has no intention on stopping the divorce or working things out with me.

"Nice to meet you," she said.

Feeling as though I was about to explode, without responding to her, I turned around and started to walk away.

"Nema! What did you need?" Al shouted after me.

I ignored him.

Without looking towards the porch, I backed out of the driveway, and sped away.

I wanted to cry, but I didn't.

Instead, I rolled down my window, and threw my wedding ring out of it.

Goodbye, Al.

Oh, and whether he knows it yet or not...

It's goodbye to Michelle, too!

~***~

"Nema, this is Benny," Vanessa beamed.

"Nice to meet you," he shook my hand. He turned his attention back to Vanessa. He kissed her, and then, he was gone.

"Whew, girl, I'm so in love with that man!" Vanessa smiled.

"I can tell," I laughed. "Love looks good on you."

"Thank you," Vanessa raised a bottle. "Tequila? Tacos?"

"Yes, to both."

I took a seat at her small kitchen table.

Vanessa's apartment doesn't match her personality at all. She's so feisty and full of life, yet her apartment is so clean and simple.

"So, my divorce from Al will be final tomorrow.

Vanessa froze. "What?'

I hadn't gotten around to telling her about my martial problems. Now, I don't really have a choice but to put it out there.

Al and I are done.

I thought he would at least try calling me all night, after I saw Michelle at his house, but he didn't.

He simply sent one text message and asked me why I'd stopped by. I thought by not replying he would call, but nope. He didn't say anything else and neither did I.

"When did this happen?"

"It's been happening for a while now. I just didn't want to say anything until I was sure that we wouldn't be getting back together."

"And? You're sure?"

"I'm absolutely sure."

I glanced at my cell phone.

4:05 p.m.

The husband auction is tonight at Lula's house at eight. And my mind and my nerves are all over the place.

"I'm so sorry, Nema. I thought you guys were okay. You guys made the cutest couple."

"Yeah. We did. He's already seeing someone else. I popped up on him yesterday, and she was at the house."

"Ouch."

"Yeah. Ouch," I exhaled. "But it's okay. It's all going to be okay." I took a shot of tequila.

"I don't think I like the way you just said that," Vanessa placed two chicken tacos in front of me.

"I was going through something, I'll admit that. You know? I wasn't sure what I wanted from one day to the next. But I expected him to fight for me. I expected Al to want me more. I just didn't expect…I just didn't think…" I took a bite of my taco. "As I said, it's okay. At least it will be."

"Was she pretty?"

"What?"

"The woman you saw at Al's. Was she pretty?"

"Yes."

"Damn. Let me get you another shot."

Vanessa and I talked for a while longer, and after seeing that it was already after five and I still needed to go to Sophie's house and get dressed, I told Vanessa that I would come by to see her again soon.

After taking a quick shower at Sophie's, I put on a beautiful, fitted red dress that I'd gotten from her boutique.

I also pulled out the new Prada pumps and purse that I'd purchased for myself with some of the money from my savings. I pulled my hair into a bun, and placed on a diamond necklace, with big dangling diamond earrings.

I wanted to look like I belonged in the room tonight.

As I painted my lips with red lipstick, I thought about what I was going to do.

Am I really doing this?

Am I really about to sell my husband?

I know this is wrong.

I know that.

A part of me just doesn't care.

And it's because of Al's actions.

Though there's no guarantee that Al will give whomever a second look, even after I make her as appealing to him as she can be, but as long as he doesn't end up with Michelle, that's all that matters to me.

She can't have him.

She can't have my husband.

Partly because I feel as though if he hadn't met her, Michelle, during our separation, maybe Al would've fought harder to keep me. He would've fought more to save our marriage.

But he didn't.

And I'm sure it's all because of her.

After placing five of my new paintings carefully in the trunk of my car, I headed towards Lula's house.

"Oooh, look at you!" Lula said immediately after opening her front door. "You look stunning!"

"Hi, Lula. You look beautiful too," I complimented her.

Lula was wearing a mahogany-colored dress, matching pumps, and gold jewelry. Her weave sew-in was freshly done, and the luxurious human hair bundles were long, stopping in the middle of her back.

"I have some paintings in my trunk."

"Oh! Carlton!" Lula screamed. A man dressed in a black uniform approached us. "Can you get the paintings out of Ms. Reid's truck?"

"Hey, now. I'm still Mrs. Montgomery for one more day."

Lula chuckled. "Indeed, you are, aren't you?"

I followed her towards an office, where a woman was seated on the couch.

"Nema, this is Margie. She's an attorney."

"Hi," I smiled at the woman, before asking my question to Lula. "An attorney?"

"Yes. Since there will be big bucks involved; I mean, who knows, the bid could reach millions. You never know. So, I believe that it's necessary to have paperwork involved. To cover you. And the buyer."

"Paperwork?" I took a seat on the couch next to the woman.

"So, we know this is an unusual scenario," the lawyer started to speak. "These papers just state that you will be getting paid an X amount, which will be filled in at the end of the auction, and these papers state that you will hold up your end of the deal by teaching, training or providing the purchaser with the necessary information on capturing the attention or interest of your soon-to-be ex-husband, Alfonzo Montgomery. These papers also state that once you are paid, you won't have a change of heart or try to sabotage the relationship between the purchaser and your ex-husband, in anyway. If they don't get together, that's fine, but you agree to answer any questions, and help in anyway that's suitable to help the purchaser with their…um…purchase."

I picked up the papers.

Slowly, I read every single word on them.

If I didn't understand something, I asked.

I'm used to paperwork being involved at the auction house, and though for whatever reason, I was caught off guard, it actually makes sense.

It is in fact a purchase.

More or less.

And the paperwork actually works in my favor too.

"If I sabotage the relationship in anyway or refuse to give information that the purchaser deems necessary in the pursuit of Mr. Montgomery, I will be in breach of contract, and therefore responsible for returning all of the money I receive," I read aloud.

"Yes," the lawyer nodded. "You would need to pay back every penny. This also applies if for some reason you change your mind about the entire, uh---process. Just return the full payment amount. If you agree to the terms, you will sign here and the winner will sign here," she pointed.

"I just tried to think ahead. Having this little contract in place will help the ladies feel more comfortable with bidding," Lula butted in. "They don't mind throwing away money. But I can assure you that they will want what they paid for."

"I understand."

"So, tell me something, Nema Montgomery…are you ready? Who knows, things can get wild, and you could leave here a millionaire tonight."

I exhaled.

A millionaire?

This isn't how I envisioned making my first million dollars, to say the least.

"These ladies have been calling about this auction all week! They're ready, Nema." Lula smiled. "Are you?"

As ready as I'll ever be.

I can't believe I'm doing this.

"Oh!" Lula interrupted my thoughts. "Let me show you the presentation cards of the ummm…the item," Lula exited the room.

"Why did you agree to do this?" Margie, the lawyer asked once Lula left the room. "He must've really pissed you off."

"Yeah. But I pissed him off first," I exhaled.

"You can change your mind. You know that, right? Right here, right now, you can decide not to do this. You can change your mind and call the whole thing off."

I nodded. "I know. I just don't know if I want to."

Lula came back into the room with the oversized poster board.

"The picture you sent me of Al," Lula turned the poster board around.

It was a picture of Al.

It's one of my favorite pictures of him.

It shows how flawless his skin is, his amazing, crooked smile, and his left dimple. It also shows just enough of his upper body.

Beside his picture, Lula had his full name, his age, his height, where he works, his annual salary, the fact that he has no kids, and three of the top qualities that she asked me for.

"Wow," I said overwhelmed. "Um, just wow."

"I know!" Lula squealed.

"Am I really doing this?"

Lula leaned up against her desk. "Are you?"

Tomorrow, my divorce will be final.

Life won't be what I thought it would be.

Al could very well run off and marry Michelle the day after tomorrow if he wants to.

It's not like things like that don't happen.

It happened to Vanessa.

And where would that leave me?

Divorced.

Unemployed.

Unsure of what the future holds for me or my career.

But tonight…

Tonight, I have the opportunity, no, I have the choice to be in control.

The choice to set myself up for better; or at these the possibility of what better may be.

The choice to believe in my dreams and actually do something about it. And the choice of possibly choosing the next woman Al ends up with.

Even if it's not necessarily my choice to have.

"Are you doing this, Nema?"

I exhaled as I stood to my feet.

"Yes."

I signed my name on the contract, and Lula poured me a drink. "Cheers to your new life. Get ready!"

An hour or so later, the women started to arrive.

I sat in a chair, on a small stage that Lula had placed in the middle of the same room she'd held the brunch.

With the picture of Al displayed beside me, I watched woman after woman be ushered into the room with a red paddle in her hand.

Twenty-two women showed up to bid on my husband. Twenty-two.

All of the women from the brunch that day, the ones who spoke to me were there. Others were new faces.

I scanned the crowd.

Out of twenty-two women, just from looking at them, only about eight of them are Al's type.

From me, to Michelle, to all of Al's exes, Al definitely has a type.

His type of woman is curvy, brown-skinned, natural hair and he loves a big ass.

Most of these women are petite. And hardly any of them were wearing their natural hair.

Five workers headed towards the stage, carrying my wrapped-up paintings. They placed them on stands behind me on the stage to showcase after Al was sold.

The ladies were all served drinks.

I was on my third drink.

I was a nervous as a chicken about to get its head chopped off.

Honestly, I just wanted to run out of the room and never look back.

"Are you okay?" Lula touched my shoulder as she reached me another glass of champagne.

"Not really," I admitted, taking a sip.

I wonder what these women think of me.

Some of them stared at me.

I could only assume that they were wondering how this whole ordeal came about. Some of them probably felt sorry for me. Maybe they pitied me and saw me as desperate.

Desperate for riches and the want to have a lifestyle like theirs.

Or maybe…

Maybe they could care less about the why I'm auctioning off my ex. Maybe they're just hopeful that they'll get the chance to be his next.

They're the ones who appear to be desperate.

Not me.

I finished the glass of champagne.

Fuck it!

Let's do this!

"Shall we begin?"

Lula stepped back. "The stage is yours. Do your thing."

I stood to my feet.

Instantly, the room fell silent.

I cleared my throat.

"Um, my name is Nema Montgomery, and I uh…" Nervously, I glanced at the photo of Al. "I have a *Husband for Sale*."

The room roared in applause and laughter.

This is just like the auction house, Nema.

I took a deep breath.

"So, let me tell you ladies a little bit about the item," I began. "My husband...ex-husband as of tomorrow, Al Montgomery is the man of every woman's dreams. He was the man of mine, that's for sure," I swallowed the lump in my throat. "He's thirty-four, smarter than any man you'll ever meet. He can fix anything, and you will never have to worry about taking out the trash. Well, I'm sure most of you don't take out your own trash anyway."

There was light chattering, but I continued.

"He sings. And he's pretty good at it too. If you ever get sick, he'll sing a special song, just for you."

Every woman in the room sang "aww" for a second or two.

"Oh, and you'll never have to pump your own gas again."

I thought about Sundays.

Every Sunday night, Al took my car to fill it up for the week. And he always left money for lunch and my favorite gum in the cupholder for me to find the next morning.

"He washes dishes, does laundry, cooks, and he likes to watch Romantic Comedies."

The women in the room cooed.

"He's funny, gives the best foot rubs, and he's a really good communicator. And shall we talk about sex?"

The women cheered as though my husband was a piece of meat.

"He likes to have sex...everyday...and I am not exaggerating. So, if you can't keep up, then move on out of the way. But I will say this...it's good sex. And I'm talking about toe curling, back breaking, bed squeaking, deep moaning type of sex. He will do anything to please you in the bedroom and outside of it too."

I almost started to cry.

Here I am, selling the perfect man to someone else, when I had him. I had him and I let him get away.

"Uh…" I fought to hold back my tears. I sniffed. "Uh, he wants kids. And he's going to make a great father someday. His parents have been married for decades and he comes from a big, family-oriented family. He loves his family. He loves his friends. And he will love his lady. Simply put…he's one hell of a guy."

I exhaled.

"Then why don't you want him? If he's so great?" A woman from the crowd yelled.

"Because I'm stupid," I answered honestly. "I felt like he was too perfect. He's the perfect husband. I tried to be the perfect wife. I tried to do everything right. I tried to do things the way I thought he would want me to. It became too much for me. Too much pressure. I lost myself. I lost my passion, for a while. I lost my happiness. He became my entire world, and I woke up one day missing the life and the world I had before he was a part of it. I wanted my old self, and my old life back. So, I pushed him away. I walked out on him. I left him. I made the biggest mistake of my life. And so, here we are. My screw up is about to set one of you up with the best man you could ever ask for. And with my help, hopefully, one of you will become the next Mrs. Montgomery."

Well, here goes nothing.

"So, let's get started, shall we?"

The ladies cheered.

And then, almost in sync, they started to wave their bidding paddles.

"We have a contract in place. All of you have been told this, correct?"

The women nodded.

"Okay. The starting price that you all agreed on is…"

Lula handed me a piece of paper.

Before the women arrived, we thought it would be a good idea to let the women choose where the bidding should begin.

I opened it.

"$50,000? Really?"

The women nodded again.

"Wow! Okay! Let the bidding begin!"

The room full of women applauded.

Some of them took big gulps of their champagne. Others appeared to be ready for war.

"For this fine, piece of a man, with great sex and a good heart…I have $50,000…do I hear $55,000?"

"$55,000!" A woman wearing a fur jacket raised her paddle.

"Okay, $55,000. Do I hear $60k?"

"$60,000!" The lady that had been wearing the red dress from the brunch waved her paddle in the air.

Keep going, Nema.

"Okay, $60k, do I hear…let's say…$75k?"

Paddles went up, over and over again.

At this rate, it seemed as though the bidding was never going to end. And then, the woman from the brunch who had been wearing the emerald ring, raised her paddled and shouted.

"$250,000!"

I almost fainted.

That alone would purchase the building for my art gallery.

"Arlene, you're not the only one who came to spend some money today," a woman that I don't remember from the brunch said. "$500,000!"

$500,000?

Is this a joke?

Half a million dollars for a man?

For a man that they aren't guaranteed to have?

For a few moments, I was unable to speak.

The room filled with chatter

"One million dollars!" I heard in between my thoughts.

And there it is.

One million dollars.

Lula assured me that tonight I could become a millionaire.

She was right.

I'm about to sell my husband for at least a million dollars. My mind started to race, thinking of all the things I could do, and buy with a million dollars.

"1.5 million!" Another woman said.

I stuttered to try in get out my words, but before I could, Lula stood to her feet.

"Two million dollars," she said.

What?

Lula is bidding?

For some reason, I expected her not to.

She and I were friends.

And we appeared to be on the road back to friendship.

Why would she bid on Al?

Why would she want to be with my ex-husband?

Lula placed a smirk on her face.

"2.5 million," a woman in a blue dress stood up. "And I'll name our first baby after you," she laughed. But her laugh was short lived.

"Three million dollars," Lula grinned. "And I'm prepared to go up to twenty."

The crowd went wild as I stared at Lula.

She smiled at me.

"I'm about to change your life!" she yelled.

Was this her plan all along?

"Uh, three million? Do I hear four?"

The women chatted amongst each other, but no one raised their paddles.

I repeated myself, hoping that somebody, anybody, topped Lula's bid.

But no one did.

"Three million going once. Three million going twice…" I hesitated. It almost killed me to say my next words. "Three million sold to the lady of the house. Lula."

Surprisingly, the entire room stood to their feet and started to clap as Lula started to bow in laughter.

Lula just bought my husband.

And I want to whoop her ass!

****

SIX

"Do you know of anyone who would want to do this to your business, Ms. Reid?"

Both Sophie and I stared at Maz.

"I can think of a few people," Sophie answered coldly.

Sophie's boutique had been completely destroyed overnight.

The door had been kicked in.

Clothes and shoes were destroyed and all over the place. Every mirror in the place had been shattered. And the cash register is missing.

Somehow, Sophie's alarm had been disabled.

And judging by the look on Sophie's face, it was obvious that she believed Maz, the Police Chief and her ex-lover, had something to do with it.

"Walk with me," he said to Sophie.

She did as she was told.

I walked around the boutique again.

Sophie has worked so hard to get to where she is, and I hate that this happened to her.

Looking at the mess, this is going to cost Sophie thousands of dollars. And who knows how long she'll have to shut down for repairs and new inventory.

"I know his stalking ass did this!" She screamed once Maz, and his employees walked out of the boutique. "He did this! Just to see me! Just to get back at me! He did this!"

I stared at Sophie, wondering if she was going to cry, but she didn't.

Sophie never cries.

Never.

If she does, it's never around anyone.

Sophie didn't even cry at the news of our parent's deaths, or at their funeral.

If I remember correctly, the last time I saw Sophie cry, she was about eight years old.

She cried because Daddy allowed me to ride in the front seat when actually, it was Sophie's turn.

I was always his favorite.

But since then, I've never seen her shed a single tear. And if you cried around her, she nearly went insane either trying to get you to feel better or trying to convince you to toughen up and do something other than cry about the problem.

"It's okay," Sophie said. "Insurance will cover everything, and everything will be okay," she exhaled. "And he's still not getting none of this ass! So, if he did this, it was all for nothing!" Sophie stormed away, and I attempted to clean up some of the mess.

With everything going on with me right now, I can't handle trying to keep Sophie from going on a rampage too.

My divorce was finalized two days ago, and I feel like shit. A big pile of horse shit, to be exact!

Especially since I've already sold Al to Lula.

Lula said that initially, she hadn't planned on joining in on the bidding. And then, she said she was actually saving Al from ending up with the woman who most likely would've won if she hadn't stepped in.

She says the lady had just gotten divorced for the third time, and that Al would've been miserable with her.

I don't give a damn what her reasoning was.

I don't like it!

Lula was my friend all through college, and I thought maybe we could pick up where we left off, especially once I had more money in my pockets.

But there's no way in hell we can be friends if she ends up dating or sleeping with my ex-husband!

The only thing that's keeping me from blowing a fuse is the fact that I know Al. And I know that it's going to take a miracle for him to fall for someone like Lula.

She's everything he hates in a woman.

I didn't want Michelle to have him, but I damn sure don't want Lula to have him either!

"Nema? You didn't hear me calling you?"

I turned around to face Sophie.

"No. Sorry. My mind was somewhere else."

"Still on Al?" She asked.

"Sort of."

"Well, you're divorced, now. You got all this good ole' freedom that you were missing. What are you going to do with it?"

"I don't know, Soph. Whatever I want, I guess."

"You bet your sweet ass you are! No regrets! You hear me? No regrets! You made your decision. Stick with it. Make the best of it. You got this! And I got you. Always. You're going to be okay."

If only I believed her.

Sophie and I cleaned up her boutique for hours.

We talked about love, men and money as we cleaned.

Once we were done, I rushed home to shower and meet Lula for dinner.

As soon as I walked into the restaurant, I noticed her hair. Lula had taken out her weave, and she was wearing her hair natural, and big…

Just like mine.

Literally.

Same side part and all.

"Hey, beautiful!" Lula stood up to greet me.

"You changed your hair."

"Yes. You like?" Lula played with her curls. "Obviously Al likes the whole natural thing that you have going on, or at least that's what he's used to, so, I figured I may as well get used to it too."

I instantly became annoyed by her comment.

"So, you're serious? You're serious about me helping you date my ex?"

"Why wouldn't I be serious?" Lula questioned. "Three million dollars is some serious money."

"Yes, but we were friends. Really good friends at that. And now, I'm supposed to teach you how to love the man I was in love with for five years?"

"What's the problem?" Lula snapped her fingers at the waiter. She ordered drinks for both of us. As soon as the waiter walked away, she smiled at me. "You didn't want him anymore. He'll be in good hands. I'll love him, just as much, or maybe even more than you did. I promise! What the two of you had is over. There's no sense in crying over spilled milk."

Lula could care less about my feelings.

That much was clear.

"It's just you were my friend. It's hard to…"

"Start spending some of that money. You'll see how easy all of this gets," Lula said. "You have enough money now to make any dream you want come true. I helped change your life. Now, you'll help me become your husband's new wife. Well, your ex-husband. If that isn't friendship, then I don't know what is."

She can't be serious right now!

Lula could tell that I was about to explode.

She exhaled loudly.

"Look, Nema, the past is the past. Al is your past. And it was your choice. You could've changed your mind about doing the auction at any time."

By the time I'd finished selling my paintings that night, Lula had already put her signature beside my name on the contract and had the three-million-dollar check in her hand.

She didn't give me a chance to tell her my thoughts or to change my mind.

"You're thinking too much about it."

"No. I'm thinking like any woman would who did something she shouldn't have done."

Lula shrugged. "What's done is done. Take yourself on a trip or buy a new purse. You'll be fine," she took a sip of her drink. "Now, tell me all the stuff about Al that you didn't say on auction day."

Lula is serious.

Dead serious.

And if it isn't obvious already…

I regret making a deal with a Gucci wearing devil.

~***~

"Do you want to have some fun?"

"Who is this?"

The man on the other end of the phone chuckled.

"Your neighbor. Todd."

"Todd? April's husband Todd?"

Todd and April were the neighbors who watched Al and I have sex in the driveway that day.

"Yes."

"Why are you calling me?"

"Me and my wife want to know if you want to have some fun."

"Excuse me?"

Before he could say anything else, I hung up.

I breathed loudly, trying to steady my heartbeat.

Pervert!

Sitting there, I realized that Todd called me once before a while back. He must have gotten my phone number from his wife, April. We'd exchanged numbers when Al and I first purchased the house, just in case of an emergency.

To my surprise, she and I never became friends.

I tried. In the beginning, I tried to be friends with her.

I would invite her out. I would try to call her just to chat. But she never really seemed interested in being my friend. She was always busy. And once, she stood me up only five minutes before she was supposed to meet me for drinks.

In two years of living next door to each other, April and I only had three or four conversations with each other.

Other than that, we simply waved and spoke in passing. I rarely ever spoke to or so much as waved at her husband.

The number started to call my cell phone again.

I blocked it.

Is this what I have to look forward to?

Husbands who call old neighbors to ask if they want to have some fun?

And wives who could care less?

A different number started to call, and assuming that it was Todd calling back again, I answered the phone with an attitude.

"Hello!"

"And on the third day, she answers."

"Huh? Hello? Who is this?"

"Germany."

Germany?

Oh, Germany!

The guy from the park.

Surprisingly, I smiled.

"I called you on the fourth day...you didn't pick up."

"Honestly, so much has been going on that..."

"That you forgot about me."

"Well, sort of. But it wasn't on purpose. And not to mention, you helped me make some money a few days ago."

"Oh, really?"

"Yes."

I sold the painting *Germany's Smile* the same night I sold my husband. It was my highest selling painting that night.

"Well, I'm glad I could be of assistance," he paused. "I haven't stopped thinking about you since that day in the park."

My heart fluttered.

"Hmmm, I know game when I hear it," I laughed.

Germany chuckled. "Then you should know that what I'm saying isn't a game. I'm looking forward to the opportunity of seeing you again."

Likewise.

But I didn't say my comment aloud.

I'm not looking for love right now.

At least, I don't think I am.

But there's something about him.

And even if it never turns into love…

A little conversation never hurt nobody.

Besides, Al has already moved on.

And not to mention, Lula is about to be hot on his trail.

A guy friend just might be what I need to keep me sane throughout all the madness.

"So…" Germany's calm voice pulled me away from my thoughts. "Have you painted anything new?"

"Actually, I was just getting settled to paint," I took a deep breath. "Would you like to join me?"

For the next three hours, Germany remained on video chat with me as I painted.

We talked.

We laughed.

We shared stories, and interests outside of art.

It felt good to have someone to talk to who seems to be truly interested in my passion.

Al supported my passion.

But I don't think he was ever extremely interested. There's a big difference.

Through conversation, I learned that Germany is a Pediatrician, which somewhat made me think of Al, because of his love for kids.

I couldn't help but wonder how many kids Germany wanted in the future, though I didn't ask. And he never mentioned having any, so, I assume that he doesn't.

Before getting off the phone, Germany made me promise that I would answer his call later on that night.

Unexpectedly, I'm all smiles.

And not to mention, I'd completed the new piece of art that I'd started on the other day, while on the phone with Germany.

A notification from the bank popped up on my cell phone.

I'd deposited the check from Lula.

I stared at my account balance.

Wow.

I'm a millionaire.

Officially.

And I feel more guilt than I'd expected to feel.

I'm sure it has something to do with Lula wanting, well, paying to be the new apple of Al's eye.

How am I supposed to deal with that?

Instead of thinking about it too long, I grabbed my purse, and headed out to do exactly what Lula suggested I do.

I'm going to spend some of the money on myself.

Maybe it will make me feel better.

After all, I could always warn Al to stay away from a woman named Lula. I'm not sure he'll listen to me, but if Lula finds out...

Wait.

What if I don't spend any of the money?

I can just give it back.

Right?

The agreement says that I'll have to pay all the money back if I don't fulfill my end of the deal or try to sabotage the progression of a possible relationship in any way.

But if I never spend any of the money...

Yes! I'll just give the money back.

With Lula's help, I sold all five of my paintings the same night I sold Al.

And Lula made sure the women paid me ten times more than what I would've charged for them, so, all together, I have a good bit of money for an art gallery, without using any of the auction money from selling Al.

I'll just give it back.

Problem solved.

Instead of going out to spend the money as planned, I asked Lula if I could come by her house.

I arrived to find her doing yoga in some type of plant-filled room.

"Hi," she breathed.

"Hey."

"Grab a mat. Join me. It's good for you."

I sat on the mat, but I had no plans on participating.

"Lula, I can't do it. I thought I could, but I can't. So, I'm here to give your money back. Every bit of it."

"I don't accept refunds," Lula laughed.

"I'm serious, Lula. I haven't spent a dime of the money. You can have it back, and I can put all of this behind me."

Lula breathed. "Sleep on it."

"What?"

"Go home, and sleep on it."

"I've thought about it, and if it was anyone else, I think I would be fine, but you and I were friends, and I just can't imagine seeing you and Al out...together."

"Sleep on it. Call me tomorrow."

And with that, Lula continued doing her yoga routine as though I wasn't there.

I don't need to sleep on it.

I thought about Lula's words as I drove away from her house.

Al isn't my husband or my concern anymore, and though I didn't want him to end up with the Michelle woman, I refuse to let Lula have him!

She was my friend.

She knows things about me that I never so much as mentioned to my husband.

I just can't allow it.

I can't do it.

My cell phone started to vibrate just as I entered the highway.

I thought it was going to be Lula, but it wasn't.

Germany.

"For a pediatrician, you sure do have a lot of time on your hands," I answered.

Germany chuckled. "People make time for what they want to make time for. Besides, I have an unexpected break, so, I was hoping to spend it by talking to you."

I blushed.

"I was just sitting here thinking about our conversation from earlier. I would love to see you again...in person," he said. "I want you to tell me all about that art gallery you were talking about opening up, and I really think you should take a trip to some of the smaller cities in Mexico. I promise you...it will change your life. Visiting those small cities, experiencing the food and culture, and embracing the people...it'll inspire you more than you could ever imagine."

"I just might do that."

"I just might offer to take you, if you'll allow me to."

The whole drive from Lula's house to Sophie's house, Germany and I talked about the world.

I was in awe just listening to him talk about all the places he has been, and things he has seen.

Both of his parents are also doctors, and he spent most of his childhood, traveling across the world with them as they helped out in other countries.

Talking to Germany is exciting.

Talking to him made me want to be more.

Our conversation made me want to do and see more.

So much more.

And with over three million dollars in my bank account, I could do just that.

I could do anything I want to do.

Hmm...

~***~

"What does it say? What does it say?" Vanessa jumped in anticipation.

"Hold your horses, lady! It doesn't say anything, yet."

I sat on the edge of the bathtub, staring at the pregnancy test in my hand.

"Am I pregnant or not?" She asked.

I exhaled once the results appeared on the screen.

"Not," I gave her the news.

Vanessa frowned.

"I'm so sorry, sweetie."

Vanessa closed the lid on the toilet and took a seat. "It's okay. I just got really excited at the thought."

"It's too soon for you and your guy to be having a baby, right?"

"Yes. It is. But when I missed my period, I just thought…"

"It'll happen when it's supposed to happen. I promise."

Vanessa smiled at me.

Suddenly, something caught her eye.

"Bitch, why are you wearing $3,000 pair of shoes?" Vanessa stood up. "Those are the new Christian Louboutin shoes. Why do you have them on your feet?"

"I just wanted to treat myself to something nice."

Needless to say, I've started spending money.

And now that I've started, I can't seem to stop!

After talking to Germany, I realized that I deserve to live my best life, and only I know what that means to me.

I deserve my art gallery.

I deserve nice clothes and nice shoes.

I deserve a new house.

I deserve to travel the world.

And that's exactly what I'm going to do!

I told Lula that I would teach her how to be me and tell her whatever it is that she wants to know about my ex-husband.

All while I live my new life of luxury.

Besides, Al will never fall for her anyway.

I know him.

Lula basically made me a millionaire for nothing.

She just doesn't know it yet.

"$3,000 on shoes just to treat yourself?" Vanessa question. "Have you started selling drugs? Or are you selling ass? Which one? Come on, you can tell me."

"Neither," I laughed. "I've just been painting like crazy, and actually selling them for thousands of dollars."

"Really?"

"Really. And I'm about to open my own art gallery. I've found a building and everything."

I'm taking Sophie's advice, and I'm going for it.

I'm chasing after my dreams, and nothing, no one can stop me.

"Oh, my God, chica! That's amazing! I'm so happy for you!"

"Thank you! I'm nervous, but I have to stop being afraid to take chances. If we don't leap, we will never know if we will fall or fly."

"That's so true. Well, I'm proud of you. I really am."

"Thanks, friend."

"Now, all we have to do is find you another husband."

"Well…"

Vanessa stared at me. "Wait, have you already met someone? Tell me everything!"

I told Vanessa about Germany.

Germany is intoxicating.

I'm completely consumed by him whenever I talk to him.

He's different.

Definitely the most interesting man I've ever met.

Germany makes me want to try new things.

He makes me want to live a life full of extravagant experiences. He has changed my view on so many things, and I like it.

And I like him.

I really, really like him.

"He keeps asking me to go on a date."

"What's the problem?"

"I don't know. I just want to make sure I'm ready."

"Give yourself time. When you're ready, you'll know it," Vanessa smiled. "But unlike you, I do have a date tonight, so I need to be getting ready."

I have plans too.

I'm meeting up with Gia and Cathy at the bowling alley.

I haven't talked to Gia about seeing her kissing Cathy's ex-husband. And I'm unsure if I should tell either of them what I saw.

It's none of my business.

And I don't want to start anything.

But on the flip side, I'm a real friend. And I feel almost obligated to tell Cathy the truth. But then, that will affect my friendship with Gia.

I have no idea what to do.

After everything that's been going on in my life lately, I don't need any more drama or problems.

And I'm all out of patience.

Thanks to Lula.

Lula is driving me crazy!

She calls me so much these days, with questions about Al, that after a certain time, I put her on the block list until the next day.

After leaving Vanessa's, and doing a little shopping, it was time for me to get dressed and head to the bowling alley to meet up with my friends.

"Nema?"

Diana called my name as soon as I got out of my car.

I haven't seen her since the day the auction house closed.

"Well, looks like life has been good to you these days," Diana looked me up and down.

"It is. How are you, Diana?"

"Fine," she said, bluntly.

Diana got into her car and sped away.

I watched her car until it disappeared.

It wasn't until that moment that I realized that Diana just might not have a single friend.

And I somewhat felt sorry for her.

"Nema!" Gia squealed at the sight of me.

I'm not sure why I agreed to come tonight knowing how uncomfortable I was going to be.

I watched Gia and Cathy laugh together like they're still the best of friends.

This is going to be harder than I thought.

"I'm so glad we could get together tonight! I've missed you ladies. And I don't want our friendship to change since none of us are married to the *Three Brown Amigos* anymore," Cathy laughed.

"Exactly! You ladies are my sisters for life!" Gia smiled. "Now, come on. I came to whoop some ass tonight!" Gia pretended to roll a bowling ball.

I forced myself to smile.

After getting our shoes, and setting up to bowl, we all ordered our first round of drinks.

"Damn, Nema! How much money did you get from Al during your divorce? You're looking really fancy tonight."

"Actually, I didn't take anything from him. I didn't want the house, and we split our joint savings account down the middle."

"How grown-up of you," Gia laughed.

"Al was good to me. There wasn't any point in doing all of that. The divorce was enough. I hurt him enough."

My words caused me to think about Lula.

I'm supposed to meet with her tomorrow.

She's taking this whole purchasing my husband thing a lot more serious than I thought she would.

She wants to know every single detail about him.

Her never-ending, random questions about Al never seem to come to an end.

"Have either of you started dating?" Cathy asked.

"Nope," Gia lied.

Immediately, I looked away from her to avoid making a face.

"What's that look about?" Cathy asked. "Are you dating, Nema?"

I took a deep breath.

"Well, I have been talking to someone. We aren't dating, yet, but we are having pretty good conversations, every now and then. He's a doctor. A pediatrician."

"Ooooh! You snagged a doctor!" Gia clapped her hands. "I bet he's fine too, isn't he?"

I nodded.

"Does he look better than Al?"

"There's only one Al," I answered her.

Though Germany is slightly more attractive than Al.

And it's something about the way he talks.

The tone of Germany's voice makes me want to rip his clothes off and lick him from head to toe.

The two women started to ask me a hundred questions, all at once. I answered a few of them.

"I can't wait to find love again," Gia said. "I'm just so ready to try again. Hopefully, things will work out better for me the second time around."

I felt as though I was about to burst.

Eventually, I did.

After my fourth drink, and because Gia wouldn't shut up about love and relationships, finally, I said what needed to be said.

"Gia, what kind of game are you playing? Cathy is supposed to be your friend. We're all friends. We're all sisters. Isn't that what you just said?"

Both of the women looked at me confused

I like these ladies, I really do.

And I don't want to lose either of them. I enjoy being both of their friend. But no one has the time to entertain lies and bullshit these days!

So…I'm telling it!

"What are you talking about?"

"I saw you. You and Jack. Holding hands and kissing. I saw you. I wasn't going to say anything because it isn't any of my business, but for you to sit here and smile in Cathy's face knowing you're sleeping with Jack is ridiculous! She's your friend. Jack is her ex-husband. We're all supposed to be friends. Remember?" I exhaled loudly.

Cathy stared at Gia.

Gia stared at me.

"Gia, what is she talking about?"

Still keeping her eyes on me, Gia spoke.

"Fine. Okay. Jack and I have been sleeping together, on and off, for almost two years."

"What!" Cathy screamed and stood to her feet.

"We didn't mean for it to happen, it just did. We didn't want to hurt you or Paul. It just happened. But we are not together. We could never hurt the two of you that way. We don't love each other. We don't want to be together. What we had was just sex."

Just as she said her last word, Cathy slapped the taste out of Gia's mouth.

"Fuck you, Gia!" Cathy shouted. "And if I hadn't just found out that I was pregnant, I would beat your ass all up and down this bowling alley. And yes, it's Jack's! Divorced and all, we still screw, almost once a week. And now, we're pregnant! We're having a baby…the one thing you could never do!" Cathy cut Gia deep with her comment, but it was all over her face that she didn't give a damn about Gia's feelings.

Cathy picked up her purse. "I never want to speak to you again! And stay the hell away from Jack! You slut!"

Cathy stormed away.

I grabbed my purse and stood up.

"I was going to tell her. I just didn't know how."

"Well, I did it for you. After all, that's what friends are for."

~***~

"You do know you don't have to try and look just like me to catch Al's attention, right?"

These days, Lula dresses like me, talks like me, wears her hair like mine, and she's wearing my favorite shade of lipstick.

"This may be my last chance at love. I have to get it right," she said.

"You really want Al to fall in love with you?"

"That's the plan." Lula took a sip of her drink.

"And if he doesn't?"

Lula shrugged. "He will. I'm going to do everything right. I'm going to do everything you say. He will."

I doubt it.

"Were you happy with your first husband? You know, before he cheated?"

Lula gulped down the rest of her drink.

"I was head over heels in love with that man. Even after I found out about the cheating," she said. "I was willing to stay with him. And not just because of the money. I actually loved him," Lula explained. "I made him go to counseling with me. I tried not to complain, about anything, because I didn't want to say the wrong thing. I just wanted my marriage to work. I tried giving him more sex and I was open to trying new things. I wanted us to fix it. I really did. But I was too late. He was already in love with her. And when a man truly loves a woman, there ain't a damn thing you can do about it. Even if you are his wife."

Lula clearly isn't over her ex-husband.

She still loves him.

It's all over her face.

It's in her voice and in her eyes.

"I was good to him. I tried to be everything he wanted me to be. In a way, I felt like he saved me. He gave me this brand-new life. He changed the way I saw the world. He made me a better woman. And I just wanted him to know how thankful I was. I tried to be a good woman. I tried to be a good wife."

"And now you want to do it all over again? You want to try to be something you're not?"

"Oh, no," Lula corrected me. "You must've misunderstood. Though, I almost forgot it for a while, I'm every bit of a damn good woman! I just need a little help catching a damn good man," she said. "That's all. Nothing more. Nothing less. I deserve a good man. And I'm going to have one, by any means necessary. Even if it costs me three million dollars. It's my ex's money anyway." Lula laughed. "My ex-husband just paid for my future husband. Hopefully. Talk about karma!"

The waiter placed our food down in front of us.

"So, I've practically memorized everything about him that you've told me. I say it's about time to run into him. Where does he usually go on weekends?"

I told Lula what she wanted to know.

In a way, I feel sorry for her.

She's so…

Desperate.

Damaged.

Lula needs a good therapist.

Not a new man.

And most definitely not a man like Al.

"How are things going with you? Are you enjoying being rich?" Lula asked. "It feels good, doesn't it?"

If I'm being honest, it does.

To feel like you'll never have to worry about money again. It does take a weight off your shoulders.

Especially since I'm using some of the money, to start my own business, to make more money.

"You're still opening your art gallery, right?" Lula asked.

"Yes. That's the plan."

"Good. You're about to step into your destiny. All you needed was a little push. And a divorce. Your marriage was holding you back. Now, you're free. Now, you're going to flourish like never before. Watch!"

Whether I want to admit it or not…

I agree with Lula.

Since leaving Al, I'm painting again. Better than ever. I'm about to open my own business. My bank account is loaded. And I've even managed to lose fifteen pounds.

Still, I don't think I'll ever be able to accept Lula and Al together.

Ever.

After dinner with Lula, I headed home to Sophie.

I felt full.

Not physically full.

Mentally and emotionally.

To be honest, I wish I could cry and share my regrets with my sister. I wish I could tell her what I've done and ask her to help me fix it.

But I know better than that.

I know that I have to keep this whole mess with Lula to myself.

"You're going out?"

"Yes. I have a date," Sophie smiled. She twirled around in her tight black dress. "How do I look?"

"Sexy! I'd screw you if I were a man," I laughed.

"Perfect!" Sophie said. "Though I won't be screwing him tonight. I really, really like this one. And I know I say it all the time, but I really do," she said. "We've been talking for weeks. We haven't had sex yet. He makes me feel like a queen. And he actually tries to get to know me. The real me. He doesn't just want me as a trophy on his arm."

"What are you going to do about your stalkers?"

"Hopefully once they get a whiff of me being in a serious relationship, they'll go away."

"Hopefully."

I sat down on her bed.

"Let me know if I'm ever in your way. I have money to move out, whenever you're ready."

"Nema, you can stay here with me forever if you want to. I love having you here." Sophie traced her lips with a black pencil. "It's a Friday night. No plans?"

"No. I'm probably just going to relax and catch up on some of my shows."

"Please play with your pussy while I'm gone," Sophie laughed. "You have a lot of built-up stress inside that needs to be released. It's all over your face."

"Sophie…go to hell!"

"What? I'm just saying. I know you've got to miss dick. If you need to borrow one, I have a drawer full of new ones. Knock yourself out."

Thirty minutes later, Sophie was gone, I had showered, and finally resting on the sofa.

I started to think about Al.

I miss Friday nights with him.

We would catch up on all of our recorded shows, eat pizza and popcorn, and have sex, at least twice, that night.

Al always made watching TV a lot more fun than it should be. He always had something to say about what was going on, and he paid attention to every moment, of every show, to be able to communicate with me effectively.

I picked up my cell phone.

Al hasn't tried to reach out to me, at all.

I'm sure it's because his new woman and her son is occupying his time.

I started to type a text message to him.

I deleted my words at least twenty times before finally just texting: "Hey."

I waited for over thirty minutes to see if he would respond.

He didn't.

So, I turned on the T.V. and started to catch up on my first show.

All of three hours later, my phone finally buzzed, but it wasn't Al.

It was Lula.

She'd sent a long paragraph text message, so I read it aloud.

"I came out to the bar on Henry Grove Road. The one you said Al goes to sometimes with his friends. And he's here! I stood right next to him, as I ordered a drink. I pretended not to notice him, but I know that he noticed me. I'm sure he did! Oh, and you were right about the cologne he wears. He smelled so good! I swear I wanted to eat him alive! Al is going to be mine! I can feel it! TTYL!"

I threw my cell phone down on the couch in frustration.

Al is going to be hers?

We'll see about that!

****

SEVEN

"I love it! I love every square foot of it!"

I walked around the building.

"I want it."

"The price is…"

"I know the price. And I want it."

I'm going to buy the building.

I'm going to open my very own art gallery, with a twist!

My art gallery will also have a bar and bistro inside of it that will serve specialty deserts and appetizers from all over the world---especially France.

It's time to take my dreams up a notch.

And thanks to my divorce from Al, I can.

Al never texted me back the other night.

And as of about three days ago, I stopped caring.

He's done.

I'm done.

We're done.

And I accept that.

The realtor told me he would e-mail me the necessary paperwork just as I walked out of the building.

"I'm going to need one hell of a business name," I mumbled, gazing over the building as I stood on the sidewalk.

I was so happy that I could…

"Nema?"

"Al?"

Al stood only a few feet away from me with a few bags in his hand.

"Wow, you look, um. You look good."

I was wearing Balenciaga from head to toe.

"Uh, thank you," I stared at him.

He looked good too.

Damn good.

Al gazed at me. "So, how have you been?"

"I've been good. Really, really, good."

Al nodded. "I can tell." He looked at the building that I was standing in front of. "Renting a space?"

"Buying it, actually."

Al looked surprised. "Wow. Uh, congratulations."

"Thank you."

There was a long awkward pause.

"I texted you. A few days ago. You didn't respond."

"Really? I changed my number a few days after the divorce was final."

"Oh," I mumbled.

"What did you say?"

"Huh?"

"You said you sent me a text. What did you say?"

"Oh, nothing important."

My heart was racing.

I just wanted to jump into his arms and kiss him.

"Well, it was nice seeing you, Nema."

Al started to walk away. Just as he brushed passed me, I mumbled softly, unsure if he would even hear me.

"I miss you," I said.

Al never stopped walking, nor did he look back at me as he said: "I miss you, too."

~***~

"What are some things I should talk about with him on the first date?" Lula asked.

"You have to get a first date first."

"Don't worry. I will." She said, confidently. "So, what are some things that I can talk about that will instantly make him feel like we have a connection? I want him to feel like we're destined to be together."

I forced myself to smile. "Well, he loves sports. All sports, especially baseball and wrestling."

Lula typed something down in her phone.

"Check."

"He loves old Western movies, and he hates the word "Whatever". He likes to go to the park. He likes to ride his bike. He will go swimming on any given day, even if it's cold outside. And fishing is the way to his heart. If you know a thing or two about fishing, that should definitely get his attention."

Since seeing Al that day, over a week ago, I've been thinking about him ever since.

I don't have his new number, but he still has mine. And he hasn't tried to call or text me, so, whether he said he misses me or not, that tells me everything I need to know.

He misses me.

But he doesn't want me back.

And I'm done holding on to the past.

If Lula wants him, she can try her best to get him.

"Check," Lula typed as I talked. "And conversation wise. What does he like to hear?"

"Words of affirmation and physical touch are both his love languages. Compliment him and make him feel smart and appreciated. He loves to be called handsome, and he likes when you show interest in what he does for a living. If you actually know what the hell he's talking about, I'm sure that will be a plus. I never did," I admitted. "And weird touches like playing with his fingers or ears. He used to love that."

I swallowed the lump in my throat.

I'm really coaching another woman on how to capture the heart of my soulmate.

"This is going to be a walk in the park!" Lula smiled. "I'm going to be so perfect for him that it'll be hard for him not to fall for me."

"We will see."

I never bothered to mention to Lula that Al is already seeing someone else.

Michelle.

So, that might make all of this a little harder than she's expecting it to be.

Oh well. She'll find out sooner than later.

Lula asked me a dozen more questions, most of them off the wall and irrelevant. Some of them, I didn't have answers to. It made me wonder why I'd never asked Al questions like: What's your biggest fear? If you had one wish, what would it be? What's the first thing you think about when you wake up in the morning?

Lula was prepared to ask Al tons of things that I hadn't. Things that would really make him think.

Al is going to like that.

Lula left the café only about five minutes before Sophie was walking in.

"Hey," Sophie greeted me.

"Hey. Is everything done at the boutique?"

"Yes. It looks like nothing ever happened," she said. "And I hid a few tiny, secret cameras all over the store. If something like this ever happens again, I'll know exactly who did it."

"Good."

Sophie ordered a sandwich and a lemonade.

"So, finally…I want you to meet my guy," she revealed.

"The new one? The one that has been taking you out almost every night? The one that has you walking around the house singing and shit?"

"Yep! That's the one," Sophie grinned. "I can't believe I'm ready to introduce him to my family---but I am. This man is different. He's everything I've been looking for, and then some."

"But is he the one?" I questioned her.

"Honestly, I think so. He just might be."

"Wow. Well, I'm down to meet yours, if you're down to meet mine."

Sophie's mouth dropped open. "You're seeing someone? When? Nema! When?" Sophie clapped in excitement.

"We've been talking for a while now. He's a pediatrician."

"Ooooh," Sophie cooed.

"He loves art, just like me. And he's been begging to take me out on a date. I'm going to say yes. And then, maybe the next date can be a double date."

"Sounds good to me!"

Sophie sipped the lemonade that was placed in front of her.

"And since we both may be in new relationships soon…I guess now it's best to tell you that I've found a house."

I pulled out my cell phone to show Sophie a picture.

"I love it!" Sophie yelled. "That's a lot of house though, just for you. Are you renting or buying?"

"Purchased," I told her. "I bought the house in cash."

Sophie's eyes widened. "With whose cash? Yours? And don't think I haven't noticed all that expensive shit you've been wearing lately."

"I've been selling the shit out of my paintings. Remember the brunch I went to that time? The one I tried to get you to come with me? Well, she's pretty wealthy and so are her friends, and after selling one of my paintings to her, everyone else wanted one too!" I told Sophie my partial truth. I plan on keeping my "Al transaction" with Lula a secret, for the rest of my life.

So, using my artwork was the best way to explain my sudden increase in funds. "She and her friends paid top dollar for my work!"

I made sure not to mention Lula's name because Sophie knows exactly who Lula is.

Sophie used to get jealous when I would rather hang out with Lula instead of her in college.

She would complain when I would go home with Lula for the weekend, instead of coming to see her.

Had Sophie gone with me to the brunch, she would know that Lula and I are back in touch. But since she didn't go, she doesn't need to know that I'm talking to Lula at all.

"I told you! Your paintings are worth millions, Nema! I told you! Just wait until you get your business up and running. Just wait until hundreds, and maybe even millions of people see your talent! You're going to be a millionaire! Sooner than you think."

Newsflash...

I already am.

I stared at the beautiful four-bedrooms, three-bathrooms house I'd purchased earlier this week.

Sophie is right.

It's a whole lot of house for just one person, but I fell in love with it as soon as I walked through the front door. Besides, you just never know what the future may hold.

"I'm really proud of you. You're newly divorced, lost your job, and yet you have managed to turn your lemons into lemonade. Hell, I didn't expect such a fast recovery from you, but nevertheless, I'm proud."

I smiled at Sophie, but my eyes were fixated on the woman who had just walked through the café door.

Michelle.

Al's Michelle.

She's so beautiful that it's sickening!

Her skin is the same shade of an oatmeal cookie, and her hair bounced as she walked as though it was as light as a feather. She smiled, glowed, like a woman newly in love.

Like a woman in love with a man like Al.

"Al's little girlfriend just walked in," I said to Sophie.

She looked behind her.

"She doesn't have a thing on you, Nema."

She's lying.

Michelle is all that and then some.

I look like an overcooked ham compared to her.

"Stop staring at her, Nema."

"I'm trying not to. She's just…"

Sophie waited for me to finish my sentence.

"She's just the type of woman that I would expect a man like Al to be with."

Michelle grabbed her bag from the cashier, and she sashayed out of the café without a care in the world.

And I was left there, jealous, that she possibly has the best part of what used to be my world.

Ugh!

I think I'm going to be sick!

~***~

"No, you didn't!"

"Oh, yes I did!" I gave my brother, Cam, the keys to his dream car; a candy-apple red Corvette.

"Nema…what….how?"

"You don't worry about the how. It's all yours! I just wanted to do something nice for you."

"Something nice for me is taking me out to dinner. This…this is…I don't know what to say."

"Just say thank you," I kissed my brother's cheek.

"Thank you, Nema."

I got into the car with Cam, and we took his new car for a spin.

"Do you still talk to Al?" I asked.

"Yes."

"Does he talk to you about his new girlfriend?"

"We don't talk about stuff like that."

"But you do know that he's dating someone?"

"I wouldn't know. I don't ask." Cam hit the gas. "You miss him, don't you?"

"Everyday. But he has moved on. And so have I."

Germany and I talk all the time, and finally, he's taking me out on our first date tonight.

"You're seeing someone? Already?"

"Al and I haven't been together for a while now. And I didn't expect to be dating so soon. It just sort of happened. But I'm okay with it. Germany is a great guy."

"Germany? What kind of name is Germany? You dating a white guy, Nema?"

"No," I laughed at my brother. "But he does seem like a really nice guy."

Cam didn't respond.

Cam and I drove around for another ten minutes or so.

My heart skipped a beat once we pulled back up at Cam's house to find Al sitting on the front porch with my brother's wife.

"Did you know he was coming over? Why didn't you tell me?"

I checked my makeup and hair.

"You didn't ask. We're going fishing."

I waited for Cam to come around to the passenger side and open my door.

I placed an awkward smile on my face.

I was unsure if I should speak to Al or just run to my car.

I gave Cam a hug, and since his wife was on the front porch, I said hello to both her and Al.

"Hello, Nema," Al said.

I gave him a half smile and started to walk away.

"Nema?" Al called after me.

He walked towards me after saying something to Cam.

My heart was beating faster than a speeding bullet.

"Uh, you have some mail over at the house. Should I just bring it by Sophie's?"

"You can. Or just trash it. It probably isn't important anyway."

I opened my car door.

"You look good," he said to my surprise.

"I know," I smirked. "I gotta' go. I have to go and get ready for a date. Nice to see you, Al."

Why did I say that to him?

I drove away from Cam's house with Al standing in the driveway, watching my car until it disappeared.

Once I turned onto the next road, I was finally able to breathe. I guess I was trying to make Al jealous from my comment, but I'm not sure why.

The reality is, Al could probably care less about me going on a date since he has Michelle.

I guess I'd wanted to see if he reacted, or did something out of the norm, but of course, he didn't.

"Hello?" I answered Lula's phone call.

"Do you think you could put a tracker on Al's car for me?"

"Say what?" I rolled my eyes at Lula's question.

"A tracker. I want to be able to locate him so I can keep up with where he's going, in order to find the perfect place and time to make myself visible to him again."

"I'm not putting a damn tracker on his car, Lula! If you want it on there, do it yourself!"

Lula laughed. "Okay, okay, okay. Fine. I'll do it myself. Or just pay someone else to do it. Would you happen to know where he is or could be right now?"

"I just saw him. He's about to go fishing with my brother."

"Thanks a ton, hun!" Lula hung up.

What in the hell have I gotten myself into?

"Ssssss!" Sophie pretended as though her hand was on fire when I stepped into the living room later that evening.

"Girl, you look hot! Sexy mama!"

"You don't think it's too much?"

"Hell no! It shows a little bit of this and a little bit of that. It's just right."

I exhaled, hoping that the buttons on the back of the red and white dress wouldn't pop off. Just then, I noticed that Sophie was only wearing a thong, with whipped cream on her nipples.

"Uhhh, should I even bother to ask?"

When Sophie realized what I was talking about she laughed. "Oh, I'm going to have a little sex while you're out," she said. "My sex can get a little loud, so I only have sex, here, when I know you're not going to be here."

"You don't have to do that, Soph. This is your house."

"I know. But like I said, sex with me can get a little loud. And it's not me! It's always the men."

I laughed at her just as the doorbell rang.

Germany is a gentleman, so he refused to let me drive to the restaurant. He wanted to pick me up.

Excitedly, Sophie's half naked ass skipped down the hallway.

I let out a deep breath and opened the front door.

"Hi," he said as soon as he saw me.

"Hey."

"Wow. You look so beautiful," he said reaching me the orange lilies.

"You're looking quite handsome yourself."

I placed the lilies on the table by the door for Sophie to put in water.

"Are you ready?"

"Yes."

Germany led me outside to his huge pickup truck, with chrome wheels.

I giggled. "I did not expect you to be driving this."

"What kind of car did you think I drove?"

"Not this."

Germany helped me into the truck and closed the door once I was comfortable in the front seat.

Okay, Nema.

Here goes nothing.

Germany and I talked and laughed the entire ride to the restaurant. He always told such exciting stories. He made me feel as though my life has been rather boring all these years.

Germany spent a month in Alaska.

He said he loved it, and that he saw more black folks there than he expected to see.

Germany has visited all fifty states in the U.S., at least once, and he says that he has interesting stories about his visit to each of them.

I'd love to hear every single story one day.

"I'm going to let you know this right now…I don't eat cute," I laughed. "I don't smack, but trust me, I'm going to eat the hell out of this food. Okay?"

Germany chuckled. "My type of woman."

The waiter took our drink orders and just as he walked away, Germany touched my hand.

"Why would anyone want to divorce someone as beautiful as you?"

Awww.

I'd avoided talking about my marriage or my divorce from Al, with Germany as much as possible.

Honestly, I don't really know what to say.

"Actually, I'm the one who wanted the divorce, initially. I lost myself in my marriage. And then, I sort of blamed him for choices no one told me to make."

"So, he wanted to stay married?"

"Yes. At first. And then, after a while, I think he grew tired of my confusion. He filed for divorce before I could."

"Do you think you would ever want to get married again?"

"Maybe. Hopefully. Since my divorce, I've truly gotten back to doing what I love to do the most. Some of my dreams are finally coming true. And honestly, I don't know if they would've if I was still someone's wife. But now that they are, maybe marriage, next time around, won't feel so much like a job or a duty. I'll be living my dream, and hopefully he will be living his. And then, together, we can come together and make a new dream that both of us can appreciate and enjoy."

Germany nodded.

"So, what about you? Why aren't you married?"

"Between college, medical school, and trying to be as much like my parents as possible, it didn't leave much room or time for marriage. A few steamy, hospital romances, but nothing too serious. Now that I've traveled and played my role in attempting to save the world, I'm ready. I'm ready for that special someone to spend the rest of my life with. I'm really looking forward to it."

As we ate and drank, Germany and I had a really good conversation. It was so easy to talk to him. He made me feel comfortable, and when I talked about my art, I loved how much he smiled and responded to let me know that he was actually listening to me.

"It's Nema, right?"

I recognized both of the women.

They'd been at Lula's house the day I auctioned off Al.

"Yes. How are you ladies doing?"

"Great," one of them answered, just as the other one said.

"Oooh, if you don't want this one, I want first dibs!" The ladies snickered as they walked away.

"Dare I even ask?" Germany said.

Nervously, I chuckled. "It's a long story."

Dinner came to an end, and as Germany drove me towards Sophie's house, I decided that I wanted to do something else.

Going from sex with Al, every day, to no sex at all has been...well, an adjustment.

I guess you truly don't appreciate something until it's gone. And that includes regular penetration, and occasional orgasms.

"I was hoping that tonight didn't have to end so soon," I said.

Germany looked over at me.

"Meaning...I don't want to go home. I want to go home with you."

Germany laughed. "Damn, I love a woman who knows what she wants!"

Twenty minutes later, we arrived at Germany's house.

And his house was everything I expected it to be.

Unlike his choice of car.

All brick, two-stories, huge yard and a chandelier on the front porch.

"Whoa!"

"Thank you," Germany smiled. He held my hand as he led me inside. "This is home," he said as soon as he turned on the lights.

Whites, grays, and navy blue danced throughout the living room area. I could tell that it was decorated by a woman. Very elegant and chic. Nothing about his living space said that a man picked it out.

"Before you ask...my mother picked everything out."

"I figured as much."

"Would you like a glass of wine?"

I stepped out of my shoes. "Nope. I would like to see you naked, though. If I'm not being too forward."

"Not at all."

Germany led me to his bedroom, which appeared to be half the top floor of his house. His master suite was the biggest bedroom I've ever seen!

His bedroom had a fireplace, a sofa, and beautiful pieces of art, just like the ones he'd told me about.

"I've been waiting all night to do this," he said, kissing my lips before I had a chance to respond.

Germany kissed me slowly, as though he was madly in love with me. As though he hadn't kissed a woman in years. His kiss gave me all the right feelings, in all the right places, causing me to turn around to allow him to unbutton my dress.

Germany kissed my back just before pulling my dress down past my hips.

I haven't slept with anyone, but Al, in five years.

What if I do something that he doesn't like?

"Are you sure about this?" Germany whispered.

I turned around to face him.

I've never wanted to do something so bad in my life!

Germany just makes you feel all warm and fuzzy, like a pair of wool socks, in the wintertime.

He makes you want him.

He makes you want to beg him to touch you.

So, I took the lead.

Instead of answering his question, I kissed him.

Slowly at first, and then full of passion with a lot of tongue. To my surprise, Germany picked me up off my feet, and without struggling to carry me, slowly, he walked towards the bed and laid me down on his navy-blue bedspread.

We didn't speak as he undressed.

Teasingly, I removed my black laced thong and bra.

I bit my bottom lip as I stared at his naked physique.

It was like a beautiful, chestnut statue, just waiting on me to paint it. Or in this case---waiting on me to fuck it.

Finally, Germany joined me in bed, and without any further ado, he pushed my knees apart, just as he got comfortable on his stomach.

"I need you to cum for me twice tonight. Okay?"

It's hot in here!

So, so, hot in here!

The next second was nothing short of heaven on earth.

His warm wet tongue flickered up against my throbbing clit, causing me to howl in pleasure.

Germany slurped and hummed as though he was enjoying a full course meal. Timidly, I placed my right hand on the back of his head. Not because he needed any help or guidance, but because I needed a little support as I started to shove my pussy in his face.

"Oooh," I moaned as Germany attempted to suck my soul from my body. And before I knew it, my body started to heat up like a Thanksgiving turkey baking in the oven overnight.

"Yes! Yes! Yes!"

Germany is ten times better at this than Al.

Al loves to eat pussy.

But his OCD won't allow him to get all sloppy and nasty with it. He eats pussy neat, and carefully, as though he doesn't want to make a mess.

Germany, on the other hand, was all over the place with his tongue. The cover underneath my ass was drenched in spit.

A few moments later, I exploded in Germany's mouth.

I attempted to catch my breath as Germany slowly slid the condom onto his hard, a little over average size dick.

With him on his knees, Germany slid me closer to him, and into position, by pulling me by my legs.

He bent my knees towards me, and then placed both of my feet flat on his chest. Slowly, he slid his hands underneath my ass, lifting it slightly, just as he pushed his dick inside of me.

Aw, hell!

He's about to fuck me into paragraph text messages, job pop-ups and cyber stalking!

I can feel it in my bones!

Germany stared at me, almost as though he wasn't enjoying himself, but his moaning and tight grip on the sides of my ass told me otherwise.

He wasn't in a rush.

He took his time.

He wanted me to feel and enjoy every, single stroke.

And I did.

I enjoyed it so much that just as he'd asked me to, I came…again.

Germany stopped and smile.

"Wait. You haven't gotten yours yet."

"I never planned to," he said. "Tonight, was all about pleasing you. I'll get mine next time."

Ahhh!

I think I'm in love!

~***~

"I still can't think of a business name."

Now, that I've purchased the building for new art gallery and bistro combo, it's time to get to work.

"Keep it simple and to the point," Vanessa said. "Don't try to be all fancy. And I meant what I said, I'm coming to work for you."

"Good. I trust you. Even though I'll have to hire someone else too because we both know…"

"Shut up!" Vanessa laughed. "I won't be lazy. I promise." Suddenly, Vanessa growled. "I've been getting private calls for the past three days. No one ever says anything when I answer. When I find out who it is, I'm going to slap the shit out of them!" She put her cell phone inside her purse. "I meant to tell you that I saw Al the other day."

"Really? Did you speak to him?"

"No. He was with a woman."

"Brown-skinned? Really pretty?"

"No. He was with some short, light-skinned chick, with a big ass. And I know we both have a nice size ass, but her ass and her hips were enormous!"

Wait a minute…

Is she describing Lula?

I haven't heard from Lula in a few days.

Our last conversation, she told me that she'd put a tracker on Al's car while he was at work.

I called her a psychopath.

All she said was that she was going to capture Al's attention and heart by any means necessary.

"I couldn't see her face because she was facing the other way, but Al happened to turn around. He sure loves a woman with a phat ass, doesn't he?" Vanessa slapped my butt.

I asked Vanessa a few more questions.

I concluded that she had to be talking about Lula.

Lula, what are you up to?

Vanessa and I talked for a while longer, and once our cars were done being washed and detailed, I called Lula as soon as I was inside my car.

"I was just about to call you!" Lula yelled in my ear. "Soooo…" Lula sang. "I have a date with Al tonight! Yay!"

Bummer.

I'd rather Michelle have Al than Lula.

I'd rather Michelle have Al than Lula.

I'd rather Michelle have Al than Lula.

I repeated the words inside my head.

"Really? Uh, were you with him the other day?"

"Yep. How do you know?"

"A friend saw the two of you together."

"So, here's what happened," Lula popped her lips. "So, I located him the other day. He was at the park. I wasn't doing anything, so, I put on some workout gear, and headed that way. I pretended to be going out there to walk the trail. He was sitting on a bench with his laptop, so, right in front of him, I stopped to tie my shoe. I made sure he got an eye full of this ass!" Lula laughed. "He actually spoke to me, first. He said he's seen me around a few times lately. I told him that I'm new to town and that I've just been trying to get out and see what this city is all about. That started the conversation," Lula stopped to catch her breath. "I left him sitting there and forced myself to walk three laps around the park. At the end of the third one, I asked him where I could get a healthy smoothie. I pretended not to know the streets. So, he offered to take me. I followed him there, and once we were there, he offered to pay for my smoothie. We ended up talking for over an hour."

Whether I want to admit it or not...

I'm jealous.

And I mean, super jealous!

"What did you guys talk about?"

"Everything that he loves. I've been researching and studying all of his interests, so, I just kept bringing different things up as though I'm interested in them too. Al was highly engaged in the conversation, and he kept saying that we have so much in common. At the end of the conversation, he asked me out on a date."

Lula was overly excited.

"So, now, I have to crush this date! I have to be perfect! I'm going to keep in mind everything you told me. Dress like you, and act like you. Make him want another date. And then, another. And so on."

I could tell that she was smiling as she talked.

She wants Al even more than I do.

Wow.

I'm admitting it.

Despite what I've done.

I still want Al.

I want him back.

I think.

"I told him that I was divorced, but I haven't told him that I'm rich. How long do you think I should wait to tell him that?"

"Tell him on your date."

Al is such a manly man, maybe Lula being rich will turn him off. I'm sure he'll feel as though he has nothing to offer her.

Wait a minute…what about Michelle?

Where will she be while he's out on a date with Lula?

"He's such a good guy, Nema. Like, he really is. I can tell. And he was the perfect gentleman. He's perfect."

Well, rub it in, why don't you!

"I can't believe you just threw him away," Lula shrugged. "Well, actually, I can. Most women would divorce their husband for a few thousands. At least you did it for millions."

Unfortunately, that decision is now number one on my list of regrets. Accepting Lula's invite to her brunch that day, is number two.

If I could turn back the hands of time, I wouldn't have gone to the brunch. I wouldn't have opened my mouth about my marital problems. And I most definitely wouldn't have sold my husband, at the time.

"I'll want your opinion on an outfit. I already know I can't be all loud and stuff. I practiced that with him while we had our smoothies. It was hard being so calm and gentle-like for over an hour. But practice makes perfect. I'm going to snag this man! I can feel it in my bones!" Lula exclaimed. "Ciao!"

Lula hung up on me.

Wow.

This is really happening.

I sold Al to Lula, and she actually managed to get him to go on a date with her.

What if he likes her?

What if he actually falls in love with her?

What if they get married and have kids?

What if...

Germany started to call, and because I knew he was calling from work, I pushed my thoughts and feelings about Al to the side for the moment.

"Hey, you," I answered.

Since having sex two weeks ago, Germany and I have been talking every day, as often as he could.

We've also had sex two more times, and each time was better than the last.

Sex with Germany is so intense, and full of passion. It's seriously like a step before making love, and I like it.

I like it a lot.

"I just wanted to hear your voice," Germany said. "You're the best part of my day."

"Aw, you're so sweet," I said. "Are you working doubles today?"

"Yes. And after here, I'll be at the hospital tonight. So, I may not get to see you until Sunday. I'll take you somewhere nice."

"I would like that."

Germany talked for another twenty minutes, or so, and then he was gone. I actually like the amount of space and time apart that comes with dating a doctor.

I still have plenty of time for myself and to focus on the things I love.

Maybe I'm more fit to be a doctor's wife.

Maybe.

Suddenly, my thoughts were back on Al.

I do feel bad, somewhat for how everything is playing out. I never expected him to actually talk to Lula, let alone ask her out on a date. And though I've been dating Germany, and saw Al with Michelle, just hearing that he was interested enough to ask Lula out has me all in my feelings.

And I don't like it.

I pulled up in front of my new house that I'm expected to start moving into this weekend to remind myself of the life I sold the man of my dreams for.

Staring at the house, I want to feel better.

I want to appreciate the choices I've made.

I want to feel a sense of peace with my decisions.

But I don't.

If I'm being honest with myself, I just…don't.

"Nema?" I heard my name being called as I pumped my gas, about thirty minutes later.

I cleared my throat once I saw him.

My ex.

Devil Dick Draco.

"Damn, girl. How have you been?"

Draco nudged me out of the way so that he could finish pumping my gas.

"I've been good. How are you?"

"I'm making it," he said. "Damn, you look good. You look like you're doing well for yourself."

"I am. Life is good."

Draco looked as though he hadn't aged a day.

"That's good," he said. "I think about you all the time. I miss you. I tell everybody that you're the one that got away."

Nervously, I laughed.

"So, are you married?"

"Divorced. You?"

"Divorced."

I couldn't help but wonder who he married.

"Single?"

"Nope," I lied, just as Draco screwed on my gas cap.

"Faithful?" He smiled.

I didn't respond.

"Take my number. If you get lonely, hit me up."

I handed my cell phone to Draco and allowed him to add his number to my contacts.

"Call me," Draco smiled as he walked away.

Once I was inside my car, I watched him get into a Range Rover. Knowing him, he'd fucked the available balance out of a lonely wealthy woman's bank account.

He was always so good at getting what he wanted.

Though every part of my body suddenly remembered how good sex with Draco used to be, I found his contact and I deleted out of my cell phone.

I have enough shit to worry about.

And I can't afford to add Draco and his dick to the list.

~***~

This painting is so pretty!

My mother was the inspiration behind it.

She was so beautiful, just like Sophie, and I'd brought her beauty back to life on the canvas in front of me.

I remember the last time I saw my mother alive.

I remember the last thing she said to me.

I even remember what she was wearing, how she wore her hair and how she smelled.

That day, hours before her death, mama was wearing a blue dress, and white shoes.

Her hair was long, and straight, resting on her back. And she smelled like flowers. She always smelled like flowers because she was always in her garden.

I'd come home from school to find her sitting outside on a blanket. She asked me about my day. I always told her that my day was okay, even if it wasn't.

And then, mama asked me to lie on the blanket with her for a while. She cracked jokes and placed a flower in my hair. She talked about her garden and a new recipe she was working on.

Then, my father called for her to ride with him to do a few errands. And just as mama stood up, she said:

"I love you, ladybug. And I mean it."

That was the last thing she said to me.

Who would've thought that their errand run would end in a deadly car crash?

"Nema?" Sophie called for me, pulling me away from my thoughts.

I sat my paintbrush on the table and made my way to Sophie.

"Nema, I want you to meet someone," Sophie said just as I entered the living room. "Nema, this is my new man! We made it official today!" Sophie squealed.

I stared at him in confusion.

"Nema, meet Benny. Benny this is my sister, Nema."

He and I just stood there, unsure of what to do.

Benny is Sophie's new man.
And my friend Vanessa's new man too!
****

EIGHT

The movers and delivery companies worked hastily to get everything into my new house.

Home.

I own my own home.

I sat on the sofa to look through Lula's text messages.

Lula's first date with Al is tonight.

And I can't do anything about it.

I've spent a good bit of the money that I got from selling Al, and with my new business taking more money than I anticipated with renovations, it would take me forever and a day, to pay Lula back if I didn't honor the agreement between us.

Unless my art gallery exceeded my expectations.

Other than that, I just don't have the money to give back to her anymore, if I breached our little contract.

The only comfort I have is that a person can only pretend to be someone else for so long before their true colors start to show.

Lula is nothing like the woman she's pretending to be and hopefully, Al gets to see her true self, before things go too far.

Hopefully.

I went through Lula's text messages.

They were all of outfits because she couldn't decide what to wear on her date.

I picked the three outfits that I thought Al would like the least and told her to choose between them.

Al has exquisite taste in clothing.

He bought clothes for me all the time.

He even helped Sophie a few times pick out outfits for her boutique. And everything he would pick, always sold out first.

One Valentine's Day, I remember coming home to find every outfit that I'd put stars by in a plus size catalogue waiting for me all over the living room.

Al had paired each outfit with a new pair of shoes, that he picked out himself.

He would do just about anything to make me happy and see me smile.

And now...

He could be about to do all of that for Lula.

Just as I was about to start my little pity-party, Sophie and Vanessa came through my front door.

"Congratulations!" Vanessa held up a bottle of wine.

Sophie started to do a little dance.

The movers stared at Sophie with eyes full of lust.

Sorry, guys.

She's taken.

But not for long.

I invited both of them over at the same time on purpose.

I'm about to break the news to them and tell them that they're dating the same man. I'm not sure how it's all going to play out, but I have to tell them.

"Thank you," I took the bottle of wine from Vanessa.

"I didn't bring you shit," Sophie shrugged. "I hope you don't mind."

I laughed. "Girl, I lived with you for months, for free. No gift necessary."

I poured all three of us a glass of wine.

After we all took a sip, I took a deep breath.

"So, I have to tell both of you something," I started.

"What is it, Nema?" Sophie questioned.

"I don't know how to say this…" I paused.

"Spit it out, chica!" Vanessa sipped her wine.

I exhaled.

"Well…both of you are dating the same man." I guzzled down the rest of my wine as they looked at each other.

"What?" Sophie asked.

"I found out the other day, when you introduced me to this mystery man that you've been talking about for a while. Well, he's the same man that Vanessa has been seeing for months. Benny. Both of you are dating Benny. The same Benny."

Sophie sat down her glass.

Vanessa poured herself more wine.

"He's been dating both of you." I repeated.

Neither of the women said a word.

"Uh, did you guys hear what I said?"

"I heard you," Sophie answered.

"And?"

"And…I'm not going to stop seeing him."

"Neither am I," Vanessa said, to my surprise.

I was in shock!

"What does that mean?" I questioned both of them.

"It means…may the best woman win," Sophie picked up her glass and drunk every drop of her wine.

"Wait, so both of you are still going to see him? Knowing that he's seeing her?" I pointed at both of them.

Sophie shrugged. "I believe he's the one."

"Yes, he is," Vanessa said. "He's the man of my dreams."

"Well, maybe you should wake up," Sophie smiled. "He and I have something that's so rare. I've dated a lot of men, and what he and I have is special."

"Likewise," Vanessa walked away.

Once Sophie noticed Vanessa on her cell phone, she hurried to get hers too.

And that was the start of it.

For the next two hours, both women cursed and fussed at Benny. Cursed and fussed at each other. I made sure they didn't come to blows, but they did come close a few times.

This was almost like Gia and Cathy all over again.

I'm always the one to spill the beans.

I almost felt bad for opening my big mouth, but Sophie is my sister. Vanessa is my friend. And I'm not about to sit around and do nothing while this one man takes advantage of both of them.

"Why didn't you tell me this the same day?" Sophie questioned.

Vanessa stared at me too.

"Oh, trust me, I was going to say something. I just had to figure out what to say. I know how both of you feel about him. And I hate that you're in this situation."

"I'm not in a situation," Sophie mumbled. "Benny and I are going to be together."

"Over my dead body!" Vanessa yelled.

"Well…that can be arranged."

The ladies started to bicker again, as I poured myself another glass of wine.

I'm going to need another bottle.

~***~

I sat in the car, staring at Al and Lula as they walked out of the restaurant.

I had a massive headache from listening to all of the arguing between Sophie and Vanessa.

Both ladies left my house, angry and mad at the world.

Yet, both still want to be with Benny.

Both women are refusing to leave him alone and agree that they have to make him choose.

I told them both to tell him to kick rocks, but they're both madly in love with him.

Who knows how all of this will play out?

Either way, someone is going to end up hurt.

I focused on Lula and Al.

Lula stood in front of him.

She barely came to his chest, even in her heels.

They appeared to be talking.

Al was wearing a shirt that I bought him for his birthday two years ago.

Who wears a gift from their ex, on a date with another woman?

The sad thing is, I know what it means for him to be wearing that shirt.

Al calls that shirt his lucky shirt.

He got a promotion in that shirt.

He wore it the day his younger sister found out her cancer was gone.

He wore that shirt whenever he had to do a pitch or presentation.

Al loves that shirt.

And if he's wearing it tonight, that means he was hoping that his date with Lula went well.

And from the looks of it, they did.

My heart shattered into a million tiny pieces as Al leaned over to kiss her.

Nooooo!

I started to pant.

Al wouldn't have kissed her if he didn't like her.

He likes her.

He actually likes her.

Well, he likes the woman she's pretending to be.

And she's pretending to be me.

Al walked Lula to a car that was most likely a rental. All of her cars are luxury cars, yet he opened the door of a small white Honda, the same model as mine, and helped her inside.

Al stood there, watching her as she drove away before making his way to his car.

With my thoughts and feelings all over the place, I sped away, heading for the house that we used to share.

I need to talk to him.

I need to say something to him.

I need to stop the mess that I've created, before it's too late.

My phone startled me as it started to ring.

Lula.

I stopped at the red light and answered the phone.

"So, I need you to teach me how to suck dick, at least in your way. I do it, but I don't like to. I'm about a five on a scale from one to ten. And Al says he loves oral sex and getting it at random moments, so, I need you to teach me."

I became as hot as hen's piss.

"Uh, you got the guy. My job is done, right?"

"No. It was just one date, silly," Lula said. "Though we are doing a picnic at the park tomorrow, my treat. But I still need your help. Your job is almost done."

Why did I do this?

The light turned green and instead of continuing to Al's house I made a U-turn.

Suddenly, I didn't see the point in going over there.

I wasn't sure what I was going to say or do, but whatever it was, it's pointless.

I did this.

And now, I have to live with it.

"So, do you deep throat? I need all the details. Don't leave anything out!" Lula said.

~***~

"Vanessa, I've been calling you. What's wrong? Are you mad at me?"

She rolled her eyes at me.

"Benny wants to be with your sister. Not me. But of course, he does! I mean look at her!" She snarled.

Vanessa attempted to close the door in my face again.

I stopped it with my hand.

"What is he saying?"

"Nothing! He won't even answer my calls anymore! We told him to choose, and he chose her," Vanessa's voice cracked. "I'm in love with him. Like, I'm so in love with him. I truly fell for him. Finally, I thought I'd found someone who was going to give me the love that I've always wanted. The love that I deserve. And your sister took him away from me!" Vanessa exhaled. "She can have any man she wants, literally, but she wants mine. She took mine. Who's going to love me now?"

Vanessa slammed her front door shut.

"Damn it, Sophie!"

I hurried to my car.

Honestly, this isn't Sophie's fault.

Benny was dating both of them.

And Sophie is just as in love with him as Vanessa is.

But I do feel bad for Vanessa.

She's been waiting for love for so long.

In a way, feeling bad for Vanessa caused me to feel somewhat bad for Lula too.

They both want love so badly.

They crave it.

They desire it.

I was them at one time in my life.

And yet, my dumb ass threw a perfectly good man to the wolves.

From what Lula has told me, she and Al have been on several dates, now, since their first date.

Lula is on cloud nine with the progress.

I feel like throwing up every time I talk to her on the phone.

I stopped by Sophie's boutique before going home to cook dinner.

Germany is coming to my house for the first time tonight.

"Hey love," Sophie smiled at me.

"Hey. I miss seeing you every day."

"I know! Nobody told you to be grown and go buy yourself a house," she chuckled. "I miss having someone to come home to."

"I'm sure that won't be a problem for long."

Sophie grinned. "Hopefully not."

"So, you are still dating Benny?"

"Of course. Why wouldn't I be?"

"For starters, he was cheating on you."

"Depends on how you look at it," she said. "We were casually dating, at first. And he said he'd been trying to cut things off with Vanessa, for a while, before it all came out, but she was just so desperate for love that he didn't want to hurt her. But he had to choose. And he chose me. He chose us. He's not seeing her anymore. And if she says they're still together, or speaking, she's lying."

"She didn't say that. She said he chose you."

Sophie smiled.

"I'm telling you---Benny is my person. He really is."

Sophie didn't feel remorseful at all.

And I guess in a way, maybe she shouldn't.

Benny made his choice.

Unfortunately, it was Sophie.

I'll just give Vanessa some time to cool down.

"He didn't even have her number saved in his phone. Maybe he did, before me. But I used to see her number pop up on his phone, some nights when we were together. I used to call her private. I didn't know it was your friend, though. I just figured it was some chick he used to deal with that wouldn't stop calling him. I mean, if she was important to him, he would've saved her number, right?"

I didn't know how to answer that question.

Changing the subject, I hung around the boutique for another thirty minutes or so, before heading out.

"Nema, hey girl!"

I turned around to see Cathy and Jack coming out of the baby clothing store, the building right beside Sophie's boutique.

I glanced down at her stomach.

Cathy is tall and lean so there was an obvious pudge in her stomach.

"What's up, Nema," Jack said.

"So, the two of you are back together?"

"Yep," Cathy smiled. "We're back together, pregnant…and remarried."

"Wow! Congratulations!"

"Thank you. It's crazy how life works out," she said. "I miss you. We should hang out soon!" Cathy smiled.

"We definitely should."

We said our goodbyes.

Seeing Cathy and Jack together obviously made me think about Gia.

I haven't spoken to Gia since the night I told Cathy the truth about her and Jack.

I haven't bothered calling her because I don't really know what to say to her. And she hasn't called me.

Instead of reaching out to Gia, I called Vanessa, just to see if she would answer her cell phone.

She didn't.

I'm not sure why she's upset with me.

I'm not the one fucking Benny.

I could've kept my mouth shut and said nothing.

I was only trying to help.

Nevertheless, Sophie seems so happy.

She's been looking for someone to truly love her and not just the way she looks, for a very long time.

It's hard not to be happy for her if she's actually found what she's been looking for with Benny.

Before I could drive away, I got a text message from Lula asking me whether Al prefers a thong or boy shorts.

I growled.

There isn't a day that goes by that I don't think about Al and Lula.

I wonder what they're talking about or doing.

And though Germany and I are getting closer and closer, it's hard not to miss what you had when someone is constantly throwing how amazing he is in your face.

The other day, Lula told me that Al took her ice skating. I always wanted to go ice skating. We never got around to it.

Lula went on and on about how Al held her hand the whole time, and how she felt so protected and taken care of.

That's Al.

That was *my* Al.

I lied to Lula and told her that Al prefers boy shorts, but really, he goes insane over a red, lace thong.

I'm not helping her get nasty with *my* husband!

I mean….my ex-husband.

Before going home, I headed to check on the renovations of my new business.

I still don't have a business name.

But I have tons of new paintings to go into my new space.

I've been painting every day.

Some days, from the time I open my eyes, until the time I go to sleep at night.

And I paint twice as much on the days that Germany is off and on the phone with me.

I'm really enjoying Germany.

That man says and does all the right things.

The conversations that we have are enlightening.

I'm surprised that I'm saying this, but if I can't have Al back, I'm very interested in seeing where things go between Germany and I.

And I can tell that he's really into me, too.

He's always talking about marriage and kids.

He says that he wants to get married on a beach and that he wants to have a little girl and name her Rayne.

For some reason, talking about having kids with Germany feels different from the conversations with Al.

I guess it's because there's no pressure. It's not something I feel like I have to do.

I arrived at my building, to find Al standing in front of it. He was standing on the sidewalk, staring at the building, or watching the men work.

Nevertheless, what in the hell is he doing here?

"Hey," I said behind him.

"Hey," he said as he turned around.

Al looked so good that I wanted to lick him.

Or suck his dick.

Maybe a little bit of both of them.

"I was just in the neighborhood. I had a meeting down the street," Al pointed. "I couldn't remember if you told me what you were opening, so I just stopped by to take a look. You know," he shrugged.

"An art gallery and bistro combo. A place where people can view and buy beautiful art, have a glass of wine and eating delicious deserts."

Al nodded. "Cool. I figured it was going to be something like that. So, you're still painting?"

"Am I? Every day, all day. I can't seem to stop myself, even if I wanted to."

"I told you, you would get it back. I knew it."

"Yeah," I exhaled. "I just want to be great. You know?"

"And you will be."

Knowing Lula could locate Al, I checked my surroundings for one of her many cars before asking my next question.

"So, how have you been?"

"I've been okay," Al answered.

"So, the pretty, brown-skinned chick that was at the house that night I showed up, um, Michelle, right? Are the two of you…"

"No. We just work together."

Huh?

I've met pretty much all of Al's co-workers, and she wasn't one of them.

"That night, she was just there going over some last-minute things with me for a project we're working on together," Al said. "And I'm sure Sophie told you that Michelle and I weren't dating."

I looked at him confused.

"Sophie? Why would Sophie tell me that you weren't dating Michelle?"

Al stared at me. "Sophie saw us at the park, one day, before you and I were divorced. Michelle had to bring her son with her to exchange a few notes with me. Sophie walked right up to me and asked me who she was. Michelle introduced herself to Sophie. She told her she was married, and that we worked together. That was it."

"Wait, a minute. Wait, a minute. You mean to tell me that Sophie knew that you weren't dating Michelle?"

"Yes. We both told her that there was nothing going on between us. Why?"

Why is the right fucking question!

Why would Sophie lead me to believe that Al and Michelle had something going on by sending me the picture of the two of them and her son?

Why wouldn't she have just told me that she spoke to them and that there was nothing going on between them?

Why would Sophie lie to me?

Oh, God!

This changes everything!

Had I known that Al and Michelle just worked together, maybe I would've fought harder to get us back on the right track. Maybe I wouldn't have signed the divorce papers. Had I known Michelle is married, and that Al didn't want to be with her, I wouldn't have been so angry at Al.

And I wouldn't have sold my goddamn husband!

What the fuck did you do, Sophie?

~***~

"Why haven't you been answering your phone?"

Sophie giggled in my ear. "Girl, Benny surprised me with a trip to the Bahamas! I'll be back in a week. I left Whitney in charge at the store. Please, if you get time, go by and check on her and my business whenever you can. I'll call you later! I love you!"

Sophie hung up before I could say another word.

What Al said to me yesterday shocked me, and I've been trying to get Sophie on the phone ever since.

After I left from Al, I went back to her boutique to confront her in person, but when I got there, her new employee said that she'd gone to lunch with her man.

And now they're in the Bahamas!

I threw my phone on my bed, just as I took a seat on the edge. I'm so pissed at Sophie that I don't know what to do with myself!

I always knew Sophie wanted a man like Al, and just a piece of what he and I had. But I never thought she would do something that could intentionally cause us to get a divorce!

I need to talk to her about it.

I need to hear her explanation.

She's my sister.

She's my best-friend.

I want to believe that Sophie didn't purposely deceive me, but the truth is, she did.

Al has no reason to lie.

If he said he spoke to Sophie that day at the park, he did just that. Sophie knew he had nothing going on with Michelle, and she allowed me to think that he did.

She tricked me into divorcing my husband!

That bitch!

Unable to sit still, I called her cell phone back-to-back, again, but Sophie never picked up the phone.

That's okay.

I'll be waiting on her ass when she gets home!

"What!" I screamed answering the phone.

"Eww! What's got your panties in a bunch?" Lula asked.

I exhaled loudly. "Nothing. What's up?"

"Well, last night didn't go as planned. I thought Al and I were going to have sex, but he seemed a little off. He seemed as though he had something on his mind. You wouldn't happen to know what it is, would you?"

Me.

Maybe.

Probably.

When I left Al, I was pretty upset.

I told him that Sophie never told me that she spoke to him at the park about Michelle. I didn't bother to tell him that she'd sent me a picture of them.

He could tell that something was wrong.

He asked, but I just told him that I had to go, and I left him standing there in confusion as I drove away.

Al was probably wondering why I was so upset, or what happened between Sophie and I.

If I'm being honest, Al has always said that he thought Sophie was jealous of me.

He would say that everyone else in the world is looking at her---while she's always simply looking at me.

Al said it was obvious to him that Sophie would much rather have my life than her own.

I thought he was crazy.

I thought that Sophie would never want to be me.

And maybe she doesn't.

But it looks as though she wanted me to be like her, at the time.

Alone.

"No. I don't know what's wrong with him, Lula. Al is very particular. Maybe he isn't ready for sex. Don't pressure him. He hates bossy, assertive women."

"I figured as much," Lula said. "Oh, remember the gynecologist? She asked me if you had new pieces available."

"Actually, I have tons."

"Really?" Lula sounded excited. "Anything I would like?"

"Maybe. I'll send you a few pictures. And as for her, I have them all in my guestroom. If she wants to come by and look at them, she's more than welcome. Or I can send you pictures of all of them."

"I'll let her know. But send me the ones you think I would be interested in."

"Don't you think you've given me more than enough of your money?"

"I haven't given you anything. I'm a paying customer," Lula laughed. "Whether I'm paying for paintings or penis. It really doesn't make a difference. I'll be waiting on the pictures."

Lula hung up.

"Whoosah!" I breathed. "Whoosah!"

Instead of going to take pictures of my paintings for Lula, I decided to go take Germany lunch.

Though he calls me while at work all the time, I've never been to his job before. But today, I'm in desperate need of being around someone who will actually listen to what I have to say.

I'm mad at my sister.

And I'm sick of Lula.

I just need some of Germany's positive words to get me through the rest of my day.

After grabbing us both a sub, I arrived at the doctor's office where Germany works.

"Hi, I'm here to see Dr. Germany Swain."

"Who?" The receptionist asked.

"Dr. Germany Swain."

"I'm sorry ma'am, but we don't have a doctor who works here by that name."

"Are you sure? He's a pediatrician."

"I'm sure," she said. "He doesn't work at this office."

Confused, I called Germany.

He didn't answer his phone, but he immediately texted me to say that he was at work.

Funny…

I'm where he told me he works!

Without responding to him, I threw the subs in the trashcan on my way out of the building.

Germany is lying to me!

Sophie lied to me!

Who is going to lie to me next?

****

NINE

"Vanessa! Please, open the door! I need my friend!"

Vanessa hasn't answered any of my phone calls or text messages in only God knows how long.

Not only have I been trying to check on her, but I've also needed her advice and positive words to help me get from one day to the next.

Most days, I feel like I'm about to explode!

Sophie hasn't answered my phone calls in about three days. And she only texts "Still Alive" once a day, and never replies to any text messages after that.

And as for Germany...

I'd asked him about his job and his employer, just to see what he said. I thought maybe I'd heard him wrong. But he told me that he worked for the same doctor's office that assured me that he didn't work there.

I plan on confronting him about his lies and cutting him off. It's just hard for me to do when he's the only one answering his phone and giving me a listening ear these days.

Despite my constant pounding, Vanessa never answered the door.

"Hey, Cam. Are you busy?"

"I'm still at work. What's up?"

"Nothing. I need a drink. I didn't want to drink alone."

"What's wrong?"

"Too much to talk about over the phone," I mumbled, just before pulling out of Vanessa's driveway.

"Well, where are you going? I'll be off in an hour."

"Probably to the bar on Congress Street."

"Okay. I'll meet you there."

I drove to the bar in complete silence.

"Fancy seeing you here," Diana said just as I sat down at the bar.

"I could say the same for you."

She raised her shot glass before downing it.

"Where else would I be?" She said.

I ordered a vodka tonic.

"Diana, you don't have many friends, do you?"

"What gave me away?" She laughed.

"You just seem...lonely."

Diana asked for another drink.

"Maybe if you were nicer..."

"Being nice doesn't get you very far these days, Nema," she said. "Nice people finish last. Or worse, they don't finish at all."

I took a sip of my drink.

"Why are you always so angry? You always seem so mad at the world."

"I'm not mad at the world. I'm mad at you," she slurred.

"Excuse me? Why are you mad at me?"

Diana chuckled. "I've been stalking you for years, Nema."

"What?"

Diana asked for yet another drink.

"What are you talking about, Diana?"

She exhaled. "You stole him from me."

"What?" I swallowed the rest of my drink. "Stole who?"

"Al."

I looked at her confused.

"Diana is my middle name. My first name is Melanie. Al and I were kind of dating each other, before he met you," she huffed. "We met at a conference, about six years ago. The company I used to work for is somewhat in competition with his employer. Anyway, we met, talked, exchanged numbers. We went on a few amazing dates. We had great sex. We talked about marriage a few times. We had all of these goals. But everything changed when he met you," she said.

My mouth was hanging wide open.

I was literally at a loss for words.

I had no idea that Diana and Al had a thing.

I'd mentioned Diana's name to Al, quite a bit over the past year. Diana is a common name. Not super common, but common enough. I'm sure it never crossed Al's mind that I was talking about the woman who he most likely called by her first name...Melanie.

"I could tell he'd met someone else. He called less and less. He was suddenly always busy on the weekends. Everything between us changed," Diana paused. "And then, one day, he called me and said what we had was over. He dropped me, for you, just like that. I've had a little problem with obsession, in the past," Diana shrugged. "So, I became obsessed with you and him. I secretly watched both of your social media accounts. I wondered what it was about you that made him choose you. I was a nice girl. Sweet. Smart.

Just like Al. I'm an engineer, for God's sake! I put my career on hold, moved an hour away from home, and took a job at an auction house for over a year, just to be around you. Just to see what it is about you. I wanted to know why Al picked you and not me."

"Diana, Al and I were together for five years."

"Don't you think I know that? I watched every day of it. Wishing that it was me. And finally, the two of you fell apart. Low and behold, you even got a divorce! And I thought, finally, I have another chance at him. Maybe we can pick back up where we left off. But nope. Before I got the nerve to approach him, he'd already started seeing someone else. The woman from the auction house that purchased that slave girl painting. Your college friend. At first, I thought she was going behind your back to make a move on your man, but I saw you out there that night, watching them, just like I was on their first date. And then after that, I saw you and her together. Now, that confused me. Obviously, you don't care about her being with Al. The questions is…why?"

Diana waited on a response.

I didn't give her one.

She ordered another shot.

"Anyway, I came to terms with how crazy I am to have moved here for absolutely no reason at all. For a man who probably hasn't had a single thought about me since the day he fell in love with you," Diana drunk her last shot. "Finally, I'm going home. I got my old job back. I miss my family. And believe it or not, I actually do have friends back home. I'm over Al." Diana stood up. She could barely maintain her balance. "I'll probably see Al, again, one day.

Most likely at some kind of conference or something. But until then, goodbye, Al!" Diana screamed. "And I think that lady, your friend, or whatever she is…I think she's just as obsessed with you as I am….well, as I was. She follows you, sometimes. Just like I do. I figured you would want to know that. Goodbye, Nema."

And with that, Diana wobbled away, tripping over her own two feet all the way out the doors of the bar.

"I see you got started without me," Cam approached me at the bar a few minutes later. My brother kissed my forehead before ordering a drink. "How are you doing? What's going on with you, Nema?"

"What isn't?" I shrugged. "I just found out that someone has been stalking me for the past year."

"What?"

I took a sip of my drink.

"Don't worry about it. I pretty sure I'll never see them again," I exhaled. "I'm going to kill your little sister," I mumbled, referring to Sophie.

"Uh, oh. What did she do this time?"

"You wouldn't believe me if I told you."

"I don't even want to know. That's between you and her," Cam picked up his glass of Hennessey. "The two of you will work it out. You always do."

I'm not so sure about that.

Cam glanced down at his cell phone.

He exhaled, loudly, before taking a sip of his drink.

"What's wrong?"

Cam looked at me. "Marriage."

"Oh, no. Please don't tell me that you're getting a divorce, too."

"Never. I'm not getting a divorce. I don't care how many men she sleeps with---I'm not giving up on her."

"Excuse me?"

I couldn't have heard him correctly.

"Venus has a problem. She's always had the same problem. And so did I. For a few years."

I waited for Cam to continue after he order another drink.

"Not that you need to know this, but I had my first piece of ass at sixteen. And before the age of seventeen, I'd slept with ten different girls. I told myself I was going to catch up with my age, and I did. But I kept going. By my second year of college, if I had to guess, I'd slept with at least a hundred random girls on campus. I loved sex. I craved a nut, or two, a day. I had to have it. Most nights, I couldn't go to sleep without having sex."

"You're not the only man who refuses to go to sleep without sex. Al was just like that."

"Maybe. But I had a problem, Nema."

I couldn't believe how open Cam was being.

He's a man of few words, when it comes to his personal life. He's very private. Even when he took Sophie and I in, after our parents died, Cam and his wife would always go on a drive whenever they needed to talk.

"One day, I met Venus. I found a girl who loved sex as much as I did. She wanted to have sex all the time. It got to the point where we were missing classes, just to have sex. It was her idea for us to go to a class for sex addicts. Honestly, once I met Venus, I didn't have the time, the need, or even the want to screw anyone else. And I was okay with that. But I went to the classes with her anyway. It was there that I learned about her childhood. I learned how ignored and unwanted she felt by her parents. And once boys started to show interest in her because of her body, sex became her strength. Sex made her feel wanted. It made her feel important."

Cam's wife, Venus, does have a nice body.

Even after having three kids, her titties are still perky, her stomach is still flat, and her booty is still round and plump.

"I fell in love with her. All of her. And she fell in love with me, too. We were perfect for each other. For years, everything was fine. We still had sex all the time. It wasn't until about three years ago that Venus started sleeping with other men."

"Oh, Cam. I'm sorry."

"She tried to stop. She did the steps. She went back to classes. And for a while, she was doing better. Until we found out that Carter isn't my son."

"What?"

"Biologically, my baby boy, isn't my child. It was her idea to test him in the first place. She said she just wanted a peace of mind, since she was fooling around with other men at the time Carter was conceived. The results gave her the opposite. Venus felt so bad for stepping out on our marriage, that she fell into depression. She started to miss work. She wasn't being much of a mother or a wife. Sex with other men was the only way to pull her out of it. Since she started sleeping around with other men, again, Venus has been able to fulfill all her regular duties."

Cam ordered yet another drink.

"And the crazy part is, she tells me every time she steps out on me," Cam mumbled. "She just sent me a text message telling me that she slept with her co-worker on her lunch break today."

"Oh, hell no! Cam, you don't deserve this! You're a good guy!" I was burning with rage. I'd had one drink to many, and I was starting to drool, but I was well aware of the words that were coming out of my mouth.

Cam is one of the good ones.

Just like Al.

And he doesn't deserve what his wife is doing to him!

"Cam, I know you love her, but how can you live like this? How can you accept what she does to you? You deserve to be with someone who knows how amazing you are. You need to be with someone who appreciates that!"

"I know what I deserve. And so does she," Cam commented. "I can help her get back on track. I can help her get to where she needs to be. We will get through this. We always do. I vowed to love her in sickness and in health. This is *her* sickness. And my love, our love, will heal her. Again." Cam smiled at me, and then, he changed the subject.

I don't like Cam's choice.

But I can't do anything about it. All I can do is respect it. And my respect for my brother just went up a level or two. Whether Cam knows it or not, he just reminded me of everything love is supposed to be.

What Cam feels for his wife is real love.

And I deserve someone to love me just like that.

I had someone who loved me just like that.

And his name is Al.

~***~

"Vanessa?"

I opened the front door still half asleep.

I couldn't help but notice how horrible she looked.

"Come on in," I said to her.

"Where are they?"

"Who?"

"You know who," she growled. "Your sister and Benny."

I took a seat on my sofa.

Vanessa stood in front of me.

"Somewhere in the Bahamas, I think. I haven't really spoken to Sophie in days. They should be coming back soon. I guess. Are you okay? Sit down. You look like you need to sit down."

Vanessa took a seat.

It wasn't until then that I noticed the pregnancy test in her hand.

Uh oh!

"I've wanted this for so long."

I glanced at the pregnancy test.

Positive.

Unlike the last pregnancy test.

Vanessa is pregnant.

"I've called Benny and texted him. He won't respond. I went by his house and his brother said he was out of town. I figured he was with her."

"Vanessa, I don't know what to say," I said softly. "But congratulations. Even if you don't have Benny, you're still going to have the beautiful baby that you've always wanted."

"I wanted it with him!" Vanessa yelled.

My phone chimed just as she started to cry.

I stared at the picture message from Sophie.

I didn't want to add fuel to a raging fire, but honesty is best for everyone right now.

"Uh, well," I started. "It doesn't look like that will happen."

I showed Vanessa the picture of Sophie and Benny, who were both wearing wedding bands in front of a "Just Married" sign on the beach.

"Are you serious?" Vanessa started to cry harder.

Sophie and Benny are married.

I tried to comfort Vanessa, but she moved away from me.

"This is so unfair! She stole him from me! That should be me in that picture with him!"

"He lied to both of you, Vanessa. This isn't Sophie's fault."

"Of course, you're going to defend your sister!"

"I'm not defending anyone, Vanessa. All of this is Benny's fault."

"I want him back! I want to be a family with him!"

Vanessa's comments caused me to think about Diana.

She was obsessed with me.

And with Al, for over five years.

She quit her job, moved an hour away from home, and started working with me, all out of obsession over a man.

All over a man that she couldn't have.

Suddenly, I started to worry about Vanessa.

And about my sister.

Thankfully, Diana's obsession didn't go but so far, but being that Vanessa is pregnant, and emotional, there's no telling what she may start to feel from day to day.

"Vanessa, you're going to be okay. You don't have to be with Benny to have this baby. This baby is a gift. One that you've been waiting to receive for a very long time."

Vanessa stood up.

"Are you stupid? Or just dumb?" She asked me. "I don't want to raise a baby on my own! I wanted this with him!" Vanessa stormed towards the front door.

"Vanessa! Wait! You shouldn't drive upset!"

"Whoa!" A voice said as soon as Vanessa opened the door. Vanessa pushed passed the woman, with me screaming her name behind her.

"Uh, you said at eleven, right? Should I come back?"

It's Lula's gynecologist friend.

I completely forgot that she was coming over to look at the paintings this morning.

"No. Come in."

She entered my house.

"Is she going to be okay?"

I watched Vanessa drive away.

"Honestly, I'm not sure."

"Cute place," Lula's gynecologist friend said.

"Thanks. I'm sure it's nothing compared to yours."

"Actually, I live on a farm."

"Oh. Really? My aunt lives on a farm."

She followed me to the bedroom that had become my in-home art studio.

"Wow! You've been busy!"

Now, I have at least seventy paintings finished!

Some are better than others.

Some are nothing shy of amazing!

Some are absolute masterpieces that are going to make me a lot of money!

"Look around. If you see something you like, let me know."

She started to look around.

"Oh, God, I love this one! The blues and the pinks. What do you call this one?"

"*Toxic Bliss.*"

For a while, she just looked without saying a word. And then she asked me a question.

"How do you know Lula, again?"

"We went to college together. We were pretty good friends, too."

She nodded her head. "And now, she's dating your ex-husband. Does that bother you?"

I wanted to answer her honestly, but she's Lula's friend. There's no question where her loyalty lies.

"Not really. What Al and I had is over."

She picked up a painting and smiled at it.

"But you do still care about him. Don't you?"

"I'm sure I always will."

Finally, she gave me eye contact. "If you care about him, get him away from Lula."

I could tell that she was serious.

"Why do you say that?"

"Lula isn't who you think she is. Or who you remember her to be. She's ruthless. She'll do anything to get what she wants. Trust me. I know."

"Most people with money are like that, if you ask me. If they want it, they pay for it."

"Kill for it too," she said.

My heart skipped a beat.

"What do you mean?"

The gynecologist practically dragged one of my paintings towards me.

"You didn't hear that from me but," she exhaled. "She's closing in on Al, so I just feel that this is something you should know. If he's as good of a man as you both proclaim him to be…get him away from her!"

The gynecologist looked around as though she was checking to make sure no one was listening.

"Lula's money came from death. Not a divorce. Lula killed her husband," she said.

My eyes felt as though they were about to pop out of my head.

"Now, she's never admitted to it, but she's made a few slip ups here and there. She definitely killed him. She just tells majority of the folks around here that she's divorced to avoid the questions. Only I used to live in L.A. too. That's where we met. Lula left L.A. months after it all went down. And then, I decided to move here to open a new office and because my soon-to-be ex-husband wanted to relive his childhood by buying a farm. Look up William Lineberger, if you don't believe me," she shrugged. "If I were you, I would get Al away from Lula. Someway. Somehow. Anyway…how much for these three?"

~***~

"I'm sure you don't want to hear this, but sex with Al was everything I thought it would be!" Lula screamed.

237

Noooo!

I'd looked up Lula's ex-husband.

The internet said William Lineberger became a millionaire from his part ownership of an oil company.

The internet also says that he died, suddenly, from a massive heart attack. An investigation into his death was opened, but the findings concluded that no foul play was suspected in his death.

So, I'm not sure why the gynecologist thinks Lula had something to do with her husband's death, but I'm sure she has her reasons.

I also found out about the 500 million dollars that was left behind for Lula. Now, I see why Lula doesn't mind just throwing money away.

What in the hell does a person do with 500 million dollars?

"I'm sorry. I know you don't want to hear about this," she said before I could say anything. "He is your ex-husband, and you did love him. I'm just so excited! Sex was the last piece of the puzzle! Now, we're exclusive! Al and I are officially dating! We're a couple! I think. And hopefully soon, we may even be married!"

I still didn't say anything.

This is all Sophie's fault!

Sophie says she's coming home tomorrow, and I can't wait. I'll finally be able to confront her about lying to me.

And as mad as I am right now, I might even punch her in the face for forcing my hand and putting me in this situation. Her lies and deceit is the cause of all of this.

All she had to do was tell me that Al wasn't dating Michelle. Yet, she mocked the situation, pushed thoughts into my head, constantly reminded me of how happy Al looked in a picture that she knew was innocent.

"Well, your job is done!" Lula said in my ear. "I won't be bothering anymore. Your services are no longer needed. You did your job. You earned that money, honey!" Lula squealed. "And of course, we shouldn't try to be friends. If we ever really were. I did a little fishing, and prying, during our conversation about his "ex-wife" and I found it weird that you never mentioned me to Al. Not even once during your marriage. Four years of a friendship, and you never told your husband about me."

There was no reason to mentioned Lula to Al because I never told him much about the woman I was in my college days. Or prior to meeting him.

I didn't want to see me as anything less than perfect.

"Anyway, I really like him. And whether he knows the real me or not, he likes me too. For his love, I can be who I am now, forever, if it means I get to keep him!" Lula laughed. "It was nice doing business with you, Nema. Enjoy your new life of luxury. And I plan on enjoying my new life of love. See you around. Or not!"

Lula hung up just as I pulled up at Germany's house.

He's been saying that he's busy working a lot lately, and finally, I'm ready to confront him with the truth.

At least I was.

After talking to Lula, I just want to go home and cry, but I forced myself out of my car anyway.

Let's get this over with.

"Uh, hello. Is Germany here?" I asked the woman who opened the door to Germany's house.

"No, he isn't." The woman stared at me. "You're her, aren't you?"

I looked at her confused.

"The woman he was paid to entertain."

"Me?"

"Yes. You. And Germany isn't his real name. My husband's name is Cortez."

"Husband?"

"Come on in. You're going to need a glass of wine."

Unsure of what was happening, I followed the woman inside the house that I've had sex with "Germany" in numerous of times.

"Red or white?"

"Both."

She chuckled. She poured us both a glass of red wine. Hurriedly, I took a sip.

"My husband gambles. Bad. He got us into a lot of debt. He lost his practice and had to take a job somewhere else. We almost lost this house. He reached out to his sister-in-law for help. She helped us. But with conditions," the woman said. "She told him that she needed him to keep you occupied while she dates your ex-husband. She said she didn't want you dwelling on past feelings or trying to get him back. She figured if you had a new male interest that you wouldn't be worried about them. So, in order for us to get a loan from her---I had to loan you my husband. At least for a little while. We really needed the money. And once she told us we didn't have to pay it back if he did exactly what she needed him to do, I had to agree. I had to make that sacrifice for our family."

As soon as she said family, two little boys came running into the sitting area. She said a few words to them, and they went running off again.

"Lula paid Germany…I mean…"

"Yep," the wife responded. "She paid him to date you. I know all about the little auction. She was planning to spend whatever she had to in order to win your husband. She wanted Germany to help push you into actually wanting to do it. And once it was done, he was to keep you entertained. She had us living in her other house, so that Germany could bring you here. She wanted everything to look believable. She said it had to feel real."

She sipped her wine.

I felt like I was about to go crazy!

Everything, and everyone around me is…

Full of lies and full of shit!

"We took down the family pictures. We made sure all of the kid's things were away. It was hard. But we did what we had to do. We did what Lula told us to do."

Lula can go straight to hell!

And I mean that with everything in me!

"My husband has slowly been trying to cut you off. That's why he's suddenly so busy. But I'm glad you showed up. I don't like her. Lula. She needs some serious help," the woman said. "She could've just loaned us the money, but she just had to get something in return. She wanted your husband. And she got him. No matter how much it cost her. She got what she wanted. But I'm glad to be able to tell you the truth. Drink up. So, I can pour you another glass."

~***~

Both of their cars were in Sophie's driveway.

I didn't want to have this conversation in front of Benny, so I called Sophie and told her I would meet her at her boutique later on that day.

She is the reason that I got into bed with the devil, Lula, and I need to take my anger out on her.

Now!

I swear I want to take some of it out on Lula too!

The wife was telling the truth.

The man I called Germany actually came home while I was there. That's why they said he didn't work at the doctor's office. I was giving them the wrong name.

He confirmed his wife's story.

And he confirmed the gynecologist's story too.

Lula was the wife of his deceased brother.

She paid him to date me.

And he too believes that Lula had something to do with his brother's death.

I feel like a fool.

Lula basically gave him all the details to "wow" me over, the same way I'd done with her to help her win over Al.

I left the married couple's house feeling disgusted, and ashamed. But I also left with payback and vengeance on my mind.

Someway, somehow, I'm going come up with the three million dollars to give back to Lula.

And then, I'm going to go get my husband back!

Between purchasing a home, a car for Cam, the building for my business, and all the renovations so far, I had just over a 1.5 million dollars left in my bank account.

Pulling out of Sophie's driveway, I spotted Vanessa's car parked down the street.

She's watching Sophie's house.

I drove right by her, as though I didn't see her.

I don't care.

She can go over Sophie's and start trouble all she wants. I have my own trouble in store for Sophie.

Apart of me wants to feel sorry for myself.

But I don't have time for that.

It's time for war!

"Everything looks so good," I complimented the workers about an hour later.

My art gallery and bistro is almost ready, although, I have half the mind to put the entire thing up for sale once the renovations are complete.

Now, I could probably sell the building for about three or four times what I paid for it. That would get me a lot closer to the three million I'll need when I attempt to take Al back from Lula.

How did I get here?

All I wanted was to do the things I love.

I just wanted to live out my dreams, but now, I'm seeing that I could've done both.

I could've figured out how to make myself happy, as well as stay married to my husband, and make him happy too.

I could've tried harder.

I could've done anything other than walk out on my marriage.

After all, what's the point in having your dreams come true, if you don't have the love of your life standing next to you?

I left the building and after running a few errands, I circled back around to Sophie's boutique.

Her new employee swore that Sophie called to say that she was on her way in, but after waiting there for almost an hour, and because Sophie wasn't answering her cell, I decided to go back to her house.

At the sight of the police cars, and ambulance trucks in front of Sophie's house, my heart dropped into the pit of my belly. I barely put my car into park before I jumped out of it and started to run in the direction of my sister's house.

Sophie!

****

TEN

"I look like a monster!" Sophie screamed.

"No, you don't. You're still beautiful. The scars will heal."

I feel somewhat responsible for what I happened to Sophie's face.

I saw Vanessa watching her house that day.

I could've stopped to talk to her, or stayed around to make sure nothing crazy happened, but I didn't because I was mad at Sophie.

Four days ago, Vanessa knocked on Sophie's door and all hell broke loose!

She told Benny that she was pregnant.

And Sophie told Vanessa that she was going to be a great stepmom to her child.

Needless to say, that sent Vanessa into a rage!

She and Sophie got into a fist fight.

Vanessa had a box cutter in her bra, and as Benny tried to pull her off of Sophie, she started to slice at Sophie's face.

She cut her three times.

Once across the forehead.

And twice on the left side of her face.

"I'm getting plastic surgery," Sophie continued to examine her face. "And I'm not dropping the charges on that crazy bitch! I don't care if she is pregnant!"

Vanessa was arrested for assault with a deadly weapon.

Her family helped her post bail, and though I wanted to go by her house so bad, I didn't.

A part of me wants to beat the shit out of her for what she did to Sophie. The other part of me just wants to hug her.

As far as we know, she didn't lose the baby.

Finally, Sophie put the mirror down.

"Oh, what was it that you wanted to talk to me about the other day? You kept saying it was important."

"Now isn't the time, Soph."

"Why not? We're just sitting here."

She's right.

Sophie is going to be just fine, so, I might as well say what I have to say and get it over with.

"Why didn't you tell me that you spoke to Al and Michelle that day at the park?"

Sophie swallowed. "Would it had made a difference?"

"Yes! It would've!" I screamed at her. "You let me believe that Al was dating her. You let me think he'd already moved on. You lied to me."

"You didn't want him, Nema. I was doing both of y'all a favor."

"A favor? By lying to me? I didn't ask you for a goddamn favor! Not when it came to my husband and my marriage!"

"You didn't want to be married to him anymore anyway!"

"So! That was for me to figure out! Not for you to keep information from me that could've changed the outcome of the whole situation!" I stood up. "Even that night she was at his house, had I known they were just co-workers…"

"Nothing would've changed! You didn't want him! And Al is a good man! Divorcing him so that he could go find happiness with someone who will actually appreciate him was the right thing to do!"

"Wow. The sad part is that you actually believe that you didn't do anything wrong." I shook my head. "You let me believe something that wasn't true. You have no idea what you've done. You have no idea what you made me do."

I grabbed my purse.

"What? What are you talking about? What did you do? Wait! I'm sorry, Nema!"

I slammed the door behind me.

I'm done talking.

I have some work to do.

I have to get Al away from Lula.

Where do I start?

I don't have a clue!

~***~

"Why did you do this?"

"Because, I miss both of you. And though what Gia and Jack did to you was wrong, you and Jack are back together, happy, married and pregnant. Can we get through this?"

"Would you be able to forgive her if she'd slept with Al?" Cathy snarled.

"Yes. I would."

That was probably a lie.

But that's what I'm going with.

"I miss our friendship. Our talks. Our dinners. Our outings. Shit, I need them! My life is a mess! And Gia, I know you're probably mad at me for telling Cathy the truth, but it was the right thing to do."

"I'm not mad at you. You're a true friend. Had the shoe been on the other foot, I probably would've done the same thing."

"So, can we all make up? Cathy? You're having a little one. Your old ass is gonna' need some babysitters. And you know that. Make up. Just don't let Gia around your man," I cracked a smile.

"Too soon, Nema. Too soon."

The women started to have a conversation with each other as I ignored the 55th call from Sophie.

Here I am preaching to them about making up, and I won't even talk to my sister.

I spotted Al and Lula holding hands in the mall yesterday. And it made me mad at Sophie all over again.

I don't know if Al and I would still be together, but I know for a fact that I wouldn't have held the auction at Lula's house, had I known that he and Michelle had nothing going on.

I thought he'd moved on.

I thought he was throwing me away like a piece of trash because he was with her.

I was angry at him.

I was hurt.

I did what I did out of pain and jealousy.

I was wrong.

And it's all Sophie's fault!

Now, Al might end up falling in love with a woman who literally paid to be on his arm.

And what if they're right?

What if Lula did have something to do with her husband's death?

Would Al become her next victim?

If something ever happens to Al, because of me, I would never be able to forgive myself.

"Nema?"

"Huh?"

"What's wrong?"

"Nothing. I was just thinking. Have either of you seen Al?"

"I have," Cathy spoke up. "You do know that he's seeing someone, right? Like actually in somewhat of a relationship?"

"Yes. I know. Good for him," I lied.

"I met her. She's okay. In a way, she seems awkward or out of place. As though she's trying to fit in. As though she's not being herself. But she seems to really be into Al."

"Is he really into her?"

"I think so. I've heard him and Jack talking about her quite a bit. He says that she comes from money. Something about an inheritance or something."

That's a lie.

"According to Jack, she's like crazy rich, and Al wasn't sure how he felt about it. Jack told him to just focus on her and not her money. You know how Al is though. He likes to be the man. I'm not sure how that will work out. But she doesn't have shit on you," Cathy winked.

"Have you seen Paul?" Gia asked Cathy, almost timidly.

Cathy stared at her for a moment.

"Yes. And he's miserable without you."

Gia didn't respond.

"Ooh, Nema, what happened to that guy you were dating?" Cathy asked.

"Turns out he was married."

"Damn. You were really feeling him, too."

"I was feeling the person he was pretending to be."

Honestly, I'm disgusted with it all.

I had sex with someone else's husband.

I swallowed what could've been a few more of their kids on numerous occasions.

I feel like a fool.

Lula's fool.

"I saw what happened to Sophie on the news," Gia mentioned. "They said it was a lover's quarrel. I know it must've been a lot for you to be torn in between your friend and your sister."

I didn't respond.

"I hope she's doing okay."

"She is. Married. Happy. She's still the same ole' Sophie."

Sophie called again just as I said her name.

After parting ways with the girls, I drove by Al's house.

Lula's green Mercedes was in the driveway.

I guess once she revealed to Al that she was rich, she was finally able to bring a little of her lifestyle to the surface.

Al's car was gone.

They're probably somewhere on a date that Al arranged.

Without thinking too much about it, I swerved into the driveway. Al never asked for my key back, so I put it in the lock and turned it.

It still works.

The house still looks exactly the same.

Just how I left it.

Just how we decorated it...

Together.

Each item came with some kind of special memory.

I touched the couch.

We literally did rock, paper, scissors in the furniture store to decide if we were bringing home the beige or the red set.

I won.

Beige can be paired with just about anything.

I continued to walk around the house.

The house was spotless.

I headed towards the basement.

I wondered what he'd done with it since it's no longer my art studio.

I turned on the light and headed down the stairs.

I smiled at the now all-black theater room.

That's what we'd planned to do with the basement, at first. I was going to use one of the spare bedrooms as my studio. We talked about an all-black room, huge theater like screen on the wall, black painted walls, big, heated reclining leather chairs, and black plush carpet.

I was onboard with the idea, but one day, I came home to find that Al had turned the basement into my art studio instead.

I took a seat in one of the chairs.

I love my new house.

But it isn't home.

This is home.

After sitting there for a while, finally, I made my way back upstairs.

"Whoa!"

I jumped.

Al was standing in the kitchen.

"What are you doing here, Nema?" Al asked.

By the way he was dressed I could tell that he'd gone somewhere romantic with Lula.

"Uh, I just…"

Lula entered the kitchen.

She and Al were wearing the same colors.

She didn't speak to me. She barely even looked at me.

"Is something wrong?"

"No. Uh, I'm sorry," I brushed past the both of them, heading for the door.

"Nema?" Al called behind me.

My heart skipped a beat.

Maybe it's because of all the romantic movies I've been watching lately, but I convinced myself that he was about to say something life changing.

But instead, Al said: "The key."

He approached me with his hand out.

I took the key off my keyring and without saying a word I placed it in his hand.

Wait…

Al somewhat held onto my hand for a second too long.

He still misses me.

He still loves me too.

I know it!

Once I was in my car, just as I started to drive away, my phone started to ring.

Lula.

"What are you doing?" She whispered. "Why were you here?"

I didn't respond.

"What are you up to, Nema? You did your part. We had an agreement."

"The agreement is invalid and void as long as I give you the three million dollars back. Correct?"

"What?"

"Answer the question. If I give you the money back, I can back out of our agreement. And do whatever I want. Right?"

"What are you talking about, Nema" Lula questioned. "And I'm sure you don't have the money to give it back."

"No. But I'll get it."

Lula was quiet for a moment.

"Are you saying you want Al back?"

I took a deep breath.

"Maybe. I just know that I don't want you to have him."

"Too bad," Lula laughed!

Too bad, my ass!

****

ELEVEN

"Nema, you have to forgive me, eventually," Sophie whined.

"No. I don't."

"I'm sorry. I should've told you, okay? I should've told you that I spoke to Al at the park that day. I should've told you that he wasn't seeing Michelle. I didn't think it would make a difference. You didn't want him anyway."

I walked away from her.

We were at my building.

The renovations are done.

And I'm totally confused.

A part of me wants to move forward with my dream and business plan. The other half of me wants to put the building back on the market to help pay off Lula.

I can't make a decision without knowing the truth.

I have to know how Al feels about Lula.

I have to know if he still loves me or if he's falling in love with her.

If he already loves her, I may just let him be, despite the fact that I'm unsure of what Lula is really capable of.

But if he doesn't love her.

If a part of him still loves me…

"What if I drop the charges against your friend? Will you forgive me then?" Sophie asked. "I just want my sister back. I just want our relationship to go back to the way it was. You're my best friend. I recently married the love of my life. And I want to share that with you. I miss you."

And at the end of her sentence, Sophie did something that I haven't seen her do in many, many years.

She cried.

"I let my own thoughts and feelings get in the way of yours. I thought you were being selfish. I didn't like how you were treating Al. I didn't like that you were throwing your marriage away," Sophie sobbed. "All I ever wanted was a love and a relationship like yours. All I ever wanted was a man to love me the way Al loved you. So, yes. I kept it from you because I felt like you didn't deserve him anymore."

"Who the hell are you to tell me who I deserve?"

"You're right. My love life was a mess. I was all over the place. I had no right. I was out of line. I'm sorry."

I stared at Sophie's scars.

They were healing just fine.

She's going to be just as beautiful as she always was in no time.

"It's funny. You ruined any small chance of my marriage working out. And now, you're married to the man that you claim is the one. What if Al truly was my *one*? What if I was just going through something? What if I just needed time to see that? You took away the chance of us working things out. I made horrible decisions based off lies and assumptions that you could've cleared up at any time." I growled at my sister. "But you know what? I'll accept your apology, under one condition. You have to help me get my *husband* back."

Sophie sniffled one last time, before wiping her face. "Why the hell didn't you just say that then?"

~***~

Sophie and her social media following has turned my life around. I don't know why I've never thought about using her to promote my paintings before.

Maybe it's because I haven't been able to paint much over the past few years, until now.

For the past seven days, Sophie has been posting my paintings to her thousands of followers.

She's been hosting somewhat of her own auction to get as many of my paintings sold as possible.

Sophie does live streams of a painting on display in her boutique. She shows off the painting, her ass and her personality, throws out a price to the world, and the first to come buy it...it's theirs!

Sold!

Just like that!

So far, in seven days, we've been able to sell twenty-six paintings.

And because customers that shop at Sophie's boutique already knows how high-end her clothing prices are, Sophie is charging big bucks for my paintings.

And who am I kidding?

They're worth it!

Almost $200,000 made so far!

"People are commenting like crazy about this one! It's a bidding war going on in my comments! Someone just posted buying it for $13,000! I told them the first to get here with the money---it's theirs!"

I told Sophie that I needed to raise at least a million dollars. I didn't tell her why, but I told her it's the start to getting Al back. She's not sure what I've gotten myself into, but she's doing what she does best to help.

Being Sophie.

"I need to run by my building. I'm meeting the appraiser there at noon."

"Wait, you're selling the building? What about your art gallery?"

"I'm just seeing how much the building is worth now. Just in case."

I arrived at my business and to my surprised, Al's car was parked in front of it.

"I'm going to have to move my business elsewhere," I said to him.

"Whenever I'm over this way, I just stop by. And I actually wanted to speak to you."

"About what?" I approached him.

"Why were you at the house that night, Nema? Is there something you want to say to me?"

I thought about my words.

"Are you happy, Al? Like actually happy?"

"I'm okay. Why?"

"I just asked."

"Why?"

"I was just wondering…"

"Wondering what? If I miss you?"

I didn't respond.

"What if I do, Nema? Then what, huh?"

I didn't know what to say.

"What do you want, Nema?"

I took a deep breath.

It's now or never.

I wanted to know how he felt about me. I wanted to know if he still loved me. Obviously, he does.

So, I answered his question.

"You. I want you."

~***~

"We were the best of friends once upon a time, so, it's only right that I warn you. Stay away from Al," Lula threatened.

She'd been waiting outside my house the morning after my talk with Al.

After admitting to Al that I want him back, he basically said that he doesn't believe me.

Al says that I don't know what I want, and that I need to be serious about us getting back together before he does anything that he might regret.

I assuming he meant that he isn't going to cut off things with Lula, until he's sure that I have my shit and my feelings together.

"What are you going to do, Lula? Kill me like you killed your ex-husband?"

Lula looked surprised.

"You didn't know I knew about that, did you?"

"My ex-husband died from a heart attack."

"So, you say."

She smiled. "He was old as hell. I'm sure fucking a twenty-three-year-old, three or four times a week, put a lot of unnecessary strain on his heart. Don't you think?"

Lula's voice was cold.

Guilty.

"And no, I'm not killing anyone. But I will tell Al the truth."

"You wouldn't."

"Oh, but I would. I'll tell him everything. I'll tell him that you sold him to me. I'll tell him that you wanted him out of your life so bad, that you held an auction to get him off of your hands. And I have a recording of the auction to prove it. And of course, proof of the signed agreement, and the $3,000,000 check that I gave you. I'll tell him everything. Do you think he would want you back? Do you think he'll be able to stand the sight of you? All he will see is that no matter how good of a husband he was to you, you sold him to the highest bidder."

I swallowed the lump in my throat.

"I'm sure he won't want anything to do with me either, but I can live with that. Can you live with him hating you? Forever?"

I stared at Lula.

And I could tell that she wasn't bluffing.

She would tell Al everything.

"Stay away from him. Open your business. Live your life. And let me live mine…with him. You led me to the well, but I did all the work. I got him. He's mine. And you're not taking him from me! I'm sure his heart will break into a million pieces watching you go up and up on the pricing to sell him. You've already broken his heart once. You wouldn't want to do it again, now would you?"

Lula placed on her sunglasses just before strutting away.

Damn it!

She's right.

Al won't want anything to do with me if he finds out the truth. He will never speak to me again.

Lula's word against mine is one thing, but all the proof is on her side. And she has a video? It never even crossed my mind that she would record that day.

I found my cell phone in my purse.

It vibrated inside my hand.

Al.

I'd just stored Al's new number the day before.

He's calling me to talk about the things that I'd said.

He's calling me to see if I'd meant my words.

He's calling me to see what's next for us.

And the answer is …

Nothing.

Al and I will never be---again.

And there's nothing that I can do to change that.

Nothing.

~***~

I stared at the man I called Germany and his family.

He played with the kids as his wife stood by smiling at them.

As alone as I feel, these days, I somewhat wish I had a child of my own. At least I would have someone around who loves me.

"Hi," Vanessa stole my focus once she sat on the bench beside me. "Thank you," she said.

She'd asked me to meet her at the park.

Sophie dropped the assault charges against her.

I didn't ask her to.

She said she wanted to.

Vanessa rubbed her belly.

Wow.

She really was pregnant.

Apart of me wondered if she was lying, but she was definitely sporting a bump underneath her tight, black t-shirt that proves she was telling the truth all along.

"I'm going to give my baby to them."

"Why?"

"I won't be able to look at this child without feeling angry. Without feeling empty. Even when I thought I was going to jail, I couldn't bring myself to get rid of it, but I can't bring myself to raise it either."

"This is what you wanted. It's what you've always wanted, Vanessa."

"No. Love and a family is what I wanted. This is not what I wanted."

Vanessa's glow was gone.

Everything that made her so spicy and unique was just…gone.

"If you're serious, about not keeping the baby, I'll take it." I surprised both myself and Vanessa once the words came out of my mouth. "Sophie and Benny don't have to know that it's your baby. No one has to know."

"You? You want kids? I thought…"

"I know. I didn't think I wanted kids, at least not right now, either. But I just need something. I need someone. I need someone to love, if that makes sense."

"Now, you of all people know that I know what you mean," Vanessa mumbled.

Al finally stopped calling me after calling and texting me for three days straight.

I never answered his calls or his text messages because there isn't anything that can say that will change the facts.

There's nothing I can do.

Even if I gave Lula the money back, she would tell Al the truth.

Now, whatever chance I had at getting him back is gone.

Once the calls stopped, Al updated his relationship status to "In a relationship" on social media.

Now, he's telling the whole world that he is in a relationship with Lula. He even posted a selfie of the two of them somewhere in the mountains.

Al is gone.

Lula won.

Lula. 1

Nema. 0

"I'll pretend to be going through the adoption process. If you are serious, I will take the baby. At least you'll know that your child is with someone you know," I mumbled.

Surprisingly, Vanessa nodded.

"Sophie and Benny can have their own damn baby."

"I wish I could drink to that," she said.

~***~

"What are you doing here?"

It's midnight and Germany---well, Cortez, is at my front door.

"I know I was paid to get to know you, but now that I know you, I can't forget you."

"Go home to your wife."

"She's knows I'm here. She thinks…she thinks I'm in love with you. And I think I am too."

I laughed aloud. "You're in love with me? You lied to me. You deceived me. And I'm no expert on love, but I know that those two things are the furthest away from love that it gets."

"I didn't think you would be so amazing," he said. "I was just trying to pay back some debt. I didn't plan on falling for you. I didn't even plan on having sex with you. I didn't think things would go that far. But they did. And I don't regret any of it," he said. "All I think about is you, Nema. You want me to get a divorce? Cool. We haven't been happy since before the kids. We thought they would fix us, but they didn't. But with you---with you, I felt alive again. How can I fix this?"

"Go home to your wife."

I started to close my front door.

"I can show you how much I care about you, if you'll let me."

"I don't want you to show me anything," I growled. "I want you to leave and never come back."

"What if I help you take down Lula? She and your ex-husband are together. What if I help you break them up?"

"How does that benefit you? What if I decide to go back to my ex-husband once it's all said and done?"

"That's a chance I'm willing to take. But if for some reason, he doesn't want you anymore...I do. I want you," he said.

~***~

"Sophie, I don't know what to say," I said to her. "Hell, there's no point in opening the art gallery. What in the hell am I going to put in it now?"

63 paintings.

Sophie sold 63 paintings on her social media.

"Okay, bitch. We're even now, right? Will you forgive me and be my sister again?"

I laughed. "Unfortunately, all of this was for nothing. Al and I will never be together again, but yes. I forgive you."

"Yay!" Sophie hugged me.

Truth be told, I forgave her a while ago.

I realized that everything happens for a reason.

Maybe this is what life is supposed to be like for me right now. Maybe Al and I were never supposed to spend the rest of our lives together.

No.

Al ended up with Lula isn't fate.

I'll never believe that.

But maybe our marriage was meant to end, no matter how it all came about.

Sophie walked away to help one of her customers. With nothing better to do, I took a seat and started to scroll social media.

"Oh, my God!"

I read through the posts that Al's mom had suddenly passed away.

"Oh, no."

I grabbed my keys and purse.

I told Sophie I had to go and a few minutes later, I was pulling up at Al's house.

Lula's car was nowhere in sight, so I rushed towards the front door.

Al opened it after my second knock.

"Al, I'm so sorry. I just saw."

"Why are you here?" He roared.

I could tell that he'd been crying.

"I'm here because I just saw the news about your mom. Are you okay? I loved her too."

"Why are you here?" Al sniffed.

"I'm here for you. I'm here for you."

Al started to break down.

I rushed to hold him in my arms.

Al cried for a long while.

I just sat there, holding him as I softly cried too.

Al loved his mama.

Hell, everyone loved her.

And knowing what it's like to lose a parent, both of them, I knew exactly what Al was feeling at the moment.

Al's cell phone was ringing off the hook.

Once, I saw Lula's face pop up, but the others were from family members and friends.

"Are you going to be okay?" I asked him.

"I don't know."

Finally, Al lifted his head to look at me.

He stared at me.

"I just wanted to come and check on you. I just had to lay my eyes on you."

Al didn't respond.

"I know I'm the last person you want to see. I just…"

Before I could get out my next word, Al kissed me.

He kissed me, softly, as my heart started to melt.

"Al?"

He continued to kiss me.

His kisses were full of passion, and maybe even love.

I kept trying to speak, but he continued to ignore me. Finally, I surrendered and started to kiss him back.

Al's hands roamed all over my body as he slipped his tongue in and out of my mouth.

I want him.

I want him bad!

"I love you," I mumbled in between kisses. I waited on Al to say the words back to me, but before he could…

The doorbell started to ring.

Al looked towards the door.

As we both struggled to catch our breath, we both stood to our feet. Al started to fix himself as he walked towards the door.

I adjusted my shirt just as he opened it.

"Hi! I just wanted to come and check on you," Lula said as she stepped inside.

She rolled her eyes at me.

I grinned at her as I made my way towards Al.

"Thanks for coming by to check on me," Al said to me. *What?*

I hadn't expected him to say that.

I'd expected him to tell Lula to leave so that we could get back to what we were doing.

Al's like or love for Lula is more serious than I thought. In that moment, I felt ashamed.

I felt used.

I felt…

I felt like the other woman.

"Anytime," I forced myself to smile at him, and then I smiled at Lula. "Bye, Lula Lineberger."

Al looked confused. "Wait, how do you know her name? Do you two know each other?"

"Ask your girlfriend," I said as I walked down the porch steps.

~***~

Al and Lula were at the funeral together.

I figured she probably told him a lie as to how I knew her full name. I sure she hadn't told Al that we used to be friends, otherwise I doubt he would be standing next to her right now.

I watched the funeral from a distance.

Al's mom was the sweetest woman I've ever met.

She will truly be missed.

She called me a few times after Al, and I separated. She told me if I ever needed her, she was just a phone call away. She also told me that I would always be her daughter. She called me once after the divorce, but I missed her phone call. I never called her back.

I wish I had.

Before the funeral ended, I left.

I'm sure Al knows I was there somewhere.

And that's all that matters.

"Can you meet me?" he said as soon as I answered my phone.

"Meet me at my house."

Germany was already there when I arrived.

"I should start calling you by your real name."

"I like it better when you call me Germany."

"What do you want?"

"I've searched high and low, and other than the suspicion that Lula had something to do with my brother's

267

death, I can't find anything that you can hold over her head."

"It's okay. Really."

"I'm sorry. I really wanted to help."

I walked towards the porch steps.

"My wife and I are getting a divorce. I moved out two days ago."

"Good for you."

He followed behind me.

"Can we start over?"

I turned to face him.

"Hi. I'm Cortez. I'm a pediatrician. I used to have my own practice, but I couldn't stay away from Vegas. I'm officially debt free, soon to be divorced, a father of two and I would love to take you out on a date."

I stared at him.

"Ger---Cortez…" I started. "I just need to be held right now. Can you hold me?"

I don't forgive him for deceiving me.

But right now, I just need someone.

Anyone.

"I can do that."

He followed me inside.

I completely undressed as soon as I was in my bedroom, and so did he. He crawled into bed behind me, and without me having to ask, he pulled me close to him.

And with the warmth of his naked body up against mine, I exhaled, just before I started to cry.

And I cried. I cried like I've never cried before.

****

TWELVE

"My marriage is over!" Sophie whined.

"Calm down, Sophie. Tell me what's wrong."

I was still trying to get used to seeing her in tears.

"Benny is going to leave me."

"Why?"

Sophie sniffled. "I can't have kids," she said. "Now, it makes sense why I've never been pregnant before."

"What? How do you know you can't have kids?"

"I got tested," Sophie took a seat beside me. "Since the night we got married, we've been having sex every single day, trying to get pregnant. I decided to go ahead and get tested because I'm impatient and it wasn't happening fast enough for me. I got the results today. I have some kind of condition. There's less than a one-percent chance that I'll ever be able to conceive. How can I tell my husband that I can't have his baby? He wants kids. Five to be exact. We agreed on five. He's going to leave me. He's going to leave me and go be a family with Vanessa," at the mention of her name, Sophie wiped her eyes. "Damn it! Had I not dropped the charges, maybe she would've gone to jail and Benny and I could've raised her baby as our own."

That's the moment I realized how selfish Sophie can be. It's always about her.

Always.

"Maybe she won't want the baby and give it to us."

The thing is…

Vanessa doesn't want the child, at all, but I dared not say that to Sophie.

"Just tell your husband the truth. He will understand."

"No. He won't. You have to see the way he lights up about having kids. He even made it clear to me that he was going to get a blood test Vanessa's baby and if it's his, he's going to be a part of the child's life. He made that crystal clear. He wants kids so bad. And now, I can't give him any. I'm not going to tell him. I can't tell him. He will leave me. I'm sure of it."

"Sophie, if you keep something like this from him and he finds out later, I can promise you that you'll lose him. Forever. And I'm sure you don't want that."

"I'm going to lose him either way."

"You don't know that. Just tell him the truth. He loves you. Everything will be fine."

Sophie started to cry again.

I held her for as long as she would let me.

A little while later, I watched Sophie drive away, with my cell phone already on my ear.

"Hello, Vanessa. Can you talk?"

~***~

A FEW MONTHS LATER...

"Time went by so fast!"

The days, weeks, and months rolled by and before I knew it, I was a day away from my grand opening.

Sweet Strokes Art & Bakery.

The man I once called Germany helped me come up with the name.

He's still around, but despite his efforts, I could never trust him again.

"I'm so proud of you!"

My siblings and I enjoyed a bottle of wine from what was initially supposed to be a small bistro but ended up being a bakery instead.

"I can't believe it's happening!"

I have 100 painting on display, ready to purchase on opening day. And a hundred more in the back, ready to replace those that sell.

For the past few months, I've been working my ass off! I've been painting all day and night.

I can't fail.

My opening has to be a success.

"I'm praying that you sell out of every single piece, sis," Cam smiled.

"She will!" Sophie said. "I have your grand opening all over my social media. It's going to be a full house!"

"I won't be able to stay the whole night," Cam mentioned. "I have somewhere to be."

"Where? Mr. Important?"

"I'd rather not say."

I stared at him. "Spill it, Cam!"

Cam exhaled. "If you must know…Al's bachelor party is tomorrow night."

My heart dropped.

Al and Lula are getting married?

Already?

It's only been a few months!

He dated me for two years before he proposed!

I'd long since blocked both of them and anyone associated with them on all of my social media accounts.

For weeks, I'd become obsessed with their every move. Then one day, Diana crossed my mind, and I realized I had become her.

So, I blocked them.

And resisted my urges to spy on them until they were no longer there.

"When are they getting married?"

"In two weeks. He has to go on a week-long business trip next week. So, he's going to do his bachelor party tomorrow night."

I tried my best not to show my emotions in front of them, but I couldn't help it. I started shaking uncontrollably, and suddenly, I was bawling my eyes out.

"It's going to be okay," Sophie said in my ear.

I wanted to snatch away from her, but I'd already gotten her back for this mess she put me in.

Sophie and Benny are currently going through a divorce.

I convinced Sophie to tell Benny that she couldn't have kids. I also convinced Vanessa to start contacting Benny again. I told her to start sending him pictures of her growing belly. I told her if she wanted to be a family with him, to go at him full blown because he wants kids, bad, and that's the one thing my sister couldn't give him.

I told her that she now has something more valuable to Benny than Sophie's beauty.

She has his child.

Vanessa took my advice.

Benny left Sophie.

And he and Vanessa are expecting a baby girl, soon.

As for Sophie and I...

Now, we're even.

And now that I know Al and Lula are getting married, I don't regret convincing Vanessa to steal Benny back from Sophie at all.

"Look, Nema. You have accomplished so much since your divorce. Tomorrow is a big day. Focus on that. What Al and Lula have going on doesn't matter."

"It matters to me!" I screamed. "He's marrying her because of me."

I should've told Al the truth.

I should've beat Lula to the punch and just told him what I did and why I did it.

He would've never forgiven me, but most likely, he wouldn't have been able to forgive Lula either.

And they wouldn't be getting married!

Maybe she's pregnant.

Maybe that's why he's marrying her so quickly.

And knowing Lula, she probably tricked him into getting her pregnant on purpose.

I thought I was getting over Al.

I've been trying to.

I've been dating. Heavily.

I really thought I was trying to move on, but now...

I have to stop this wedding!

After drying my eyes, my siblings helped me do one last walk through to make sure everything was ready for tomorrow.

I struggled with whether or not I should go by Al's house after leaving *Sweet Strokes*.

Popping up and telling him not to marry Lula, and telling him why, seemed like the only thing I could do.

My mind raced as I tried to decide on my next move.

And just as I decided to head Al's way, my cell phone started to ring.

It was Cathy.

I'm sure Cathy knew about the upcoming wedding.

Why hadn't she told me?

Or maybe she's calling to tell me now.

I answered her call in a hurry.

"Hello? Hello?"

"God mommy…it's time!"

"Aw, she's so beautiful!" I squealed, the next morning at the hospital.

"Pick her up. She won't bite," Cathy smiled.

I picked up the baby.

"Sierra Si'nema Parker, meet your god mommy, Nema."

My heart started to melt.

"Si'nema?"

"Yes. These past few months you have been everything to me. Thank you for helping me get through them," Cathy said.

She's right.

In order to keep myself busy, when I wasn't painting, or out with some random man, I was going above and beyond for everyone in my life these past few months.

If they needed me, I was there.

I rocked the baby, slowly.

I want one.

I want a baby too.

"Hey, hey, hey!"

I looked towards the door at the sound of his voice.

Al froze at the sight of me holding the baby.

"What's happening, bro?" Jack greeted him with a hug as he took the gifts out of his hand. "You know I won't be able to make it tonight, right?"

Al didn't answer him.

He continued to stare at me.

"Al?"

"Oh, yeah man. I definitely understand."

I glanced at Cathy.

Her eyes were locked on me.

I reached the baby to Jack instead of reaching her to Al directly.

"Aw, hi there baby girl. It's your god father, Al."

Of course, they would make him the god father.

Cathy touched my hand.

I smiled at her. "I'm going to let you get some rest. Call me when you can." I kissed her forehead and rushed out of the room.

"Nema!"

I'd only taken about ten steps before Al called my name.

I turned around as he walked closer to me.

"I heard about your grand opening tomorrow," he said.

"I heard about your upcoming wedding," I answered.

Al seemed uncomfortable. "I just wanted to say…" he paused. "Congratulations, Nema."

"Ditto."

I cried the whole walk to my car, but once I got inside, I took a deep breath and dried my eyes.

I'm going to be just fine.

Everything is going to be okay.

I got my passion back.

I got a new business.

And all I want is for Al to have the one thing he wants the most…

Love.

Maybe he has that with Lula.

I'm about to have everything I've ever wanted, too.

And sometimes that means letting go of the old things and making room for new things to come.

I drove away from the hospital, unsure of my future, but ready for whatever life brings my way.

Goodbye Al.

~***~

"Look at this shit," Sophie showed me her cell phone as she took another shot.

I was already aware of what she was showing me.

Vanessa and Benny had their baby today.

"That should've been me!" Sophie asked for another shot.

I didn't respond.

"It's not fair! It's not fair!"

"We can't always have it all, Sophie."

I shrugged as I took a sip of my drink.

"You know what, it's okay! It's all okay! I'm sexy. And beautiful. And I'm going to find me a rich man who can pay one of the top doctors in the world to help me have a baby. Watch!" Sophia downed her new shot. "Benny was the one. He really was. I married my one true love. Next time around, I'll marry for all the other shit that people marry for. Fuck love!"

I raised my glass. "Fuck love!"

Since my grand opening, over two weeks ago, life for me has changed.

My business is doing even better than I expected.

I'm painting like a crazy person to make sure I can keep up with the demand.

I sold out on the day of my grand opening.

I literally sold out of everything.

All 200 paintings.

I also sold out of every single sweet treat and every bottle of wine.

It was more than a success!

It was my destiny!

"Hey, beautiful," I heard behind me just as I placed my glass down on the bar.

The man standing behind me almost reminded me of Germany.

Germany, or Cortez, no longer bothers me.

He divorced his wife, but he realized that he was never going to have me. He was never supposed to have me in the first place. And eventually, he just stopped trying.

I glanced at Sophie to see that she was now entertaining a guy wearing a Rolex.

"You wanna' get out of here?"

Fuck love.

Fuck marriage.

Fuck complicated emotions and unnecessary feelings.

I'm exactly where I'm supposed to be in my life.

Newly wealthy.

Super single.

Very drunk.

And about to go have sex with a man who's name I probably won't even remember.

Life is good.

I guess.

~***~

"I hear the Beloved Teresa is the best pastry in town."

I stopped breathing at the sound of his voice.

Al.

I had my cell phone turned off.

His wedding day was yesterday, and I didn't want to see anything, or hear anything about it.

I spent the whole day at the beach.

I stayed at a hotel and drove back this morning.

Instead of going home, I came here, to the park, where I've been for the past three hours.

"You named a desert after my mother?"

"I loved her, too."

Al sat down on the park bench beside me.

"If someone had told me that this is how things would be between us right now, I would've never guessed it."

I didn't respond.

I was trying my best not to look at him in the eyes.

"My wedding day was yesterday," he started. "I was all set to marry a woman who came into my life as a surprise. A woman who has made everything these past couple of months…better. We have so much in common that I was almost convinced that we were destined to be together. But just as I pulled up at the church, I realized something. I realized that no matter how much I wanted her to be…she just isn't you."

I looked at Al.

He was smiling, and his eyes were swollen with tears.

"No matter how much love she had to give, no matter how much money she has, my life doesn't make sense without you. It doesn't have meaning without you in it," Al said. "You're my one. You're my person. And I've always known it. I let anger and pride get the best of me. I thought by filing for the divorce, it would help you to realize that you were losing me. In the end, I lost the one thing that matters to me the most. I lost you. I lost us. I lost…"

Before Al could finish his sentence, I kissed him.

I kissed him like never before.

"I'm sorry. And if you give us another chance, I will never give up on us again," I whispered in his ear.

"You promise?"

"I promise."

Al kissed me softly, slowly, and for what seemed like hours.

"I would like to try a *Beloved Teresa,*" Al stood up and reach for my hand.

"Okay."

Just as I stood up, my cell phone started to ring.

At the sight of her name, I felt frightened for some reason or another.

Lula.

"He loves you. I was perfect. I was everything he could've ever asked for, and he still loves you," she said.

I grabbed Al's hand with my free hand, while quietly listening to what she had to say.

I glanced around the park's parking lot.

I saw one of Lula's cars parked right beside mine.

"It's a good thing that he left me at the altar for you, so to speak, versus leaving me on down the line after we were married," she said. "I hear that a heart attack is a terrible way to die."

That's it!

Her comment clearly suggests that she actually did kill her deceased husband because of his affair.

"You got the money. You got the man. But you know what they say: All is fair in love and war. But some battles never end. Maybe one day, we'll meet again. Goodbye, Nema Reid."

Lula hung up.

"Is everything okay?" Al asked, as I watched Lula's car as she drove away.

"Yes. Everything is perfect."

"Was that Lula?"

My heart dropped. I was unsure of how to respond.

"I know the two of you aren't telling me something," Al said. "And it's fine. I don't want to know. I don't care. All I want is you."

Marriage is a lot of things.

It's beautiful.

It's sweet.

But one thing it isn't and will never be is easy.

Sometimes things fall apart just to come back together again. And sometimes things happen to push you closer towards a beautiful, blissful end.

But if ever there was a piece of advice about marriage that I could give, it would be one thing for sure.

Ladies…Before you say, *I do*.

Ask yourself this question: "How much could your husband be worth to you?"

THE END